A Christmas Garland

A Christmas Garland

A Novel

Anne Perry

BALLANTINE BOOKS • NEW YORK

Published in the United States by Ballantine Books, an imprint of The Random House Publishing Group, a division of Random House, Inc., New York.

BALLANTINE and colophon are registered trademarks of Random House, Inc.

ISBN 978-0-345-53074-5

Printed in the United States of America

Text design by Julie Schroeder

For all those who keep hope alive
in the darkness

A Christmas Garland

*L*ieutenant Victor Narraway walked across the square in the cool evening air. It was mid-December, a couple of weeks before Christmas. At home in England it might already be snowing, but here in India there would not even be a frost. No one had ever seen snow in Cawnpore. Any other year it would be a wonderful season: one of rejoicing, recalling happy memories of the past, and looking forward to the future, perhaps with a little nostalgia for those loved ones who were far away.

But this year of 1857 was different. The fire of mutiny had scorched across the land, touching everything with death.

He came to the outer door of one of the least-damaged parts of the barracks and knocked. Immediately it was opened and he stepped inside. Oil lamps sent a warming yellow light over the battered walls and the few remnants of the once-secure occupation, as they had been before the siege and then its relief. There was little furniture left whole: a bullet-scarred desk, three chairs

that had seen better days, a bookcase and several cupboards, one with only half a door.

Colonel Latimer was standing in the middle of the
room. He was a tall and spare man well into his forties;
a dozen Indian summers had burned his skin brown,
but there was little color beneath it to alleviate the weariness and the marks of exhaustion. He regarded the
twenty-year-old lieutenant in front of him with something like an apologetic look.

"I have an unpleasant duty for you, Narraway," he
said quietly. "It must be done, and done well. You're new
to this regiment, but you have an excellent record. You
are the right man for this job."

Narraway felt a chill, in spite of the mild evening.
His father had purchased a commission for him, and he
had served a brief training in England before being sent
out to India. He had arrived a year ago, just before the
issue of the fateful cartridges at Dum Dum in January,
which later in the spring had erupted in mutiny. The
rumor had been that the bullets were coated with animal grease, in the part required to be bitten into in
order to open the cartridge for use. The Hindus had
been told it was beef fat. Cows were sacred, and to kill

one was blasphemy. To put cow fat to the lips was damnation. The Muslims had been told it was pork fat, and to them, the pig was an unclean animal. To put that grease to your lips would damn your soul, although for an entirely different reason.

Of course, that was not the only cause of the mutiny by hundreds of thousands of Indians against the rule of a few thousand Englishmen employed by the East India Company. The reasons were more complex, far more deeply rooted in the social inequities and the cultural offenses of a foreign rule. The bullets had merely been the spark that had ignited the fire.

Also it was true, as far as Narraway could gather, that the mutiny was far from universal. It was violent and terrible only in small parts of the country. Thousands of miles remained untouched by it, lying peaceful, if a little uneasy, under the winter sun. But the province of Sind on the Hindustan plains had seen much of the very worst of it, Cawnpore and Lucknow in particular.

General Colin Campbell, a hero from the recent war in the Crimea, had fought to relieve the siege at Lucknow. A week ago he and his men had defeated 25,000 rebels here at Cawnpore. Was it the beginning of a turning of the tide? Or just a glimmer of light that would not last?

Narraway stood to attention, breathing deeply to calm himself. Why had he come to Latimer's notice?

"Yes, sir," he said between his teeth.

Latimer smiled bleakly. There was no light in his face, no warmth of approval. "You will be aware of the recent escape of the prisoner Dhuleep Singh," he went on. "And that his guard, Chuttur Singh, was hacked to death in the course of Dhuleep's escape?"

Narraway's mouth was dry. Of course he knew it; everyone in the Cawnpore station knew it.

"Yes, sir," he said obediently, forcing the words out.

"It has been investigated." Latimer's jaw was tight, and a small muscle jumped in his temple. "We know Dhuleep Singh had privileged information regarding troop movements, specifically regarding the recent patrol that was massacred. We also know the man could not have escaped without assistance." His voice was growing quieter, as if he found the words more and more difficult to say. He cleared his throat with an effort. "Our inquiries have excluded every possibility except that he was helped by Corporal John Tallis, the medical orderly." He met Narraway's eyes. "We will try him the day after tomorrow. I require you to speak in his defense."

Narraway's mind whirled. There was a chill like ice in the pit of his stomach. A score of reasons leaped to his mind why he could not do what Latimer was asking of him. He was not even remotely equal to the task. It would be so much better to have one of the officers who had been with the regiment during the siege and the relief do it, someone who knew everyone. Above all, they should have an officer who was experienced in military law, who had defended men dozens of times and was known and respected by the regiment.

Then a cold, sane voice inside assured him that it was precisely because he was none of these things that Latimer had chosen him.

"Yes, sir," he said faintly.

"Major Strafford will be here any moment," Latimer continued. "He will give you any instruction and advice that you may need. I shall be presiding over the court, so it is not appropriate that I should do it."

"Yes, sir," Narraway said again, feeling as if another nail had been driven into the coffin lid of his career.

Major Strafford's dislike of him dated back to the time before he had joined the regiment. Almost certainly it stemmed from Narraway's brief acquaintance with Strafford's younger brother. They had been in the same final year at Eton, and little about their association had been happy.

Narraway had been academic, a natural scholar and disinclined toward sports. The younger Strafford was a fine athlete but no competition for Narraway in the classroom. They existed happily enough in a mutual contempt. It was shattered one summer evening in a magnificent cricket match, nail-bitingly close, with Strafford's team having the slight edge—until Narraway showed a rare flash of brilliance in the only sport he actually enjoyed. The dark, slender scholar, without a word spoken, bowled out the last three men on Strafford's team, including the great sportsman himself. The fact that he did it with apparent ease was appalling, but that he did not overtly take any pleasure in it was unforgivable.

And Strafford Minor had never been able to exact his revenge on the field, which was the only place he could redeem his honor. Other victories did not count. And practical jokes or barbed wit looked to be nothing more than the spite of a bad loser.

But that was boyhood, two years ago and thousands of miles away.

"Captain Busby will prosecute," Latimer was going on. "The evidence seems simple enough. You will be free to interview Corporal Tallis at any time you wish, and anyone else you feel could be helpful to your defense. If there are any legal points that you need to clarify, speak to Major Strafford."

"Yes, sir." Narraway was still at attention, his muscles aching with the effort of keeping complete control of himself.

There was a brief knock on the door.

"Come," Latimer ordered.

The door swung open and Major Strafford came in. He was a tall, handsome man in his early thirties, but the echo of Narraway's schoolfellow, so much his junior, was there in the set of his shoulders, the thick, fair hair, the shape of his jaw.

Strafford glanced at Latimer.

"Sir." He saluted, then, as he was given permission, relaxed. He regarded Narraway expressionlessly. "You'd better read up on the case tonight and start questioning people tomorrow morning," he said. "You need to be sure of the law. We don't want anyone afterward saying that we cut corners. I presume you appreciate that?"

"Yes, sir." Narraway heard the edge of condescension in Strafford's voice and would dearly like to have told him that he was as aware as anyone else of how they would all be judged on their conduct in the matter. More than that, the future of British rule in India would be flavored by reports of decisions such as this. The whole structure of Empire hung together on the belief in justice, in doing things by immutable rules and a code of honor that they themselves never broke.

Thousands of men were dead already, as well as women and children. If the British ever regained control and there was to be any kind of peace, it must be under the rule of law. It was the only safety for people of any color or faith. Otherwise there was no hope left for anyone. Right now there seemed to be little enough in any circumstances. Delhi had fallen, Lucknow, Agra, Jhelum, Sugauli, Dinapoor, Lahore, Kolapore, Ramgarh, Peshawar—and on and on. The list seemed endless.

"Good," Strafford said curtly. "Whatever you think

you know, you'd better come and see me and tell me at least the outline of your defense." He looked at Narraway closely, his blue eyes curiously luminous in the light of the oil lamp. "You must be sure to mount some defense—you do understand that, don't you? At least put forward a reason why a man like Tallis should betray the men he's served beside all his career. I know he's a quarter Indian, or something of the sort, but that's no excuse."

The tight muscles in his face twitched. "For God's sake, thousands of soldiers are still loyal to their regiments and to the Crown, and fighting on our side. Tens of thousands more are going about their duties as usual. No one knows what the end of this will be. Find out what the devil got into the man. Threats, bribery, got drunk and lost his wits? Give some explanation."

Narraway felt dismay turn to anger. It was bad enough that he was picked out to defend the indefensible; now Strafford required him to explain it as well.

"If Corporal Tallis has an explanation, sir, I shall offer it," he replied in a hard, controlled voice. "I cannot imagine one that will excuse his conduct, so it will be brief."

"The explanation is not to excuse him, Lieutenant," Strafford said acidly. "It is to help the garrison here feel as if there is some sense in the world, some thread of reason to hold on to, when everything they know has turned into chaos, the people they love are slaughtered, and the nation on every side is in ruins." A flush spread up his fair face, visible even in this wavering light. "You are here to satisfy the law so that we do not appear to have betrayed ourselves and all we believe in, not to excuse the damned man! I know you are new here, but you must have at least that much sense!"

"Strafford . . ." Latimer said quietly, interrupting for the first time. "We have given the lieutenant a thankless task, and he is quite aware of it. If he isn't now, he will be when he has looked at it a trifle more closely." He turned to Narraway again. "Lieutenant, we do not know where we shall be by the turn of the year, here or somewhere else, besieged or comparatively free. This matter must be dealt with before then. The women and children need a celebration, however meager. We need hope, and we cannot have that without a quiet conscience. We cannot celebrate the birth of the Son of God, nor can we ask His help with confidence, if we do so with dishonor weighing us down. I expect you to conduct Tallis's defense in such a manner that we have no stain on our conduct to cripple us in the future. Do I make myself clear?"

Narraway took a deep breath and let it out slowly. "Yes, sir," he said, as if he had some idea in his head how to do it. It was a lie, by implication. He had no idea whatsoever. He saluted and left the room.

He walked away from the command building without any notion where he was going. It was totally dark now, and the sky was burning with stars and a low three-quarter moon. There was sufficient light to see the broken outline of the walls and the black billows of the tamarind trees, motionless in the still air. His feet made no sound on the dry earth.

He passed few other people, even on the road beyond the entrenchment. Sentries took no notice of him. In his uniform he passed unquestioned.

Half a mile away, the vast Ganges River murmured and shifted in the moonlight, reflecting on an almost unbroken surface, streaked here and there only when the current eddied.

The prisoner who had escaped and the guard who

had been savagely murdered in the process were both Sikhs. That in itself was not extraordinary. The Sikhs had been on both sides during the mutiny. India was made up of many races and religions, languages and variations in culture from region to region. Internal wars and squabbles abounded.

John Tallis was British, but one set of his grandparents had been Indian—Narraway had no idea, though, if they had been Hindu, Sikh, Jain, Muslim, or something else. He dreaded meeting the man; yet, as soon as he had any clarity in his mind as to how he should approach the subject, he must do it.

The crime had been monstrous, and there could be no defense. The guard, Chuttur Singh, had been hacked to death. It had not even been a simple breaking of his neck or cutting his throat, which, while gruesome, would at least have been quick. The massacre of the patrol was equally bloody, but it was, in a sense, part of war and so to be expected. But it would not have happened had the enemy not known exactly where to find the patrol and at what hour. When Dhuleep Singh had escaped, he had passed that information over.

What had changed John Tallis from a first-class medical aide, a man of compassion and loyalty, into a man who could betray his own?

Narraway was walking slowly, but already he was at the beginning of the street that led into the battered and bedraggled town. In the distance he could see the spires of two of the churches against the skyline. Nearer him, there were a couple of shops with their doors closed. There was hardly anyone around—just a glimpse of light visible here and there from a half-shuttered window, a sound of laughter, a woman singing, the smell of food. The air was chilling rapidly with the darkness. If he stood still, he would become aware of the cold.

He started to walk again, smelling the dampness of the river as he got closer to it. The earth was softer under his feet.

What did Latimer really expect of him? He had implied that he required Narraway to find something that would make sense of Tallis's act. Because people needed to understand, because no one could fight chaos. Maybe a lack of reason is man's last and worst fear, the one against which there are no weapons?

Was Latimer—as the man in command, the one everybody looked toward—trying to create a belief in order, a reason to fight?

Narraway went through the last trees and stared across the surging water, away to the northeast, where he knew Lucknow was, beyond the horizon. Exactly a month before Christmas, General Havelock had died outside the city, worn out, beaten and bereaved. Had he finally felt the consuming darkness of loss and panic and been overwhelmed by it, unable to see hope?

How much is morale affected by the character of a leader? It was a question Narraway had asked himself many times, both at school and, later, in his military training. An officer must know his tactics, must understand both his own men and his enemy, must be familiar with the terrain and with the weapons, must guard his supply lines, must gain all the Intelligence of the enemy that he possibly can. Above all he must earn the trust and the love of his men. He must act decisively and with honor, knowing what he is fighting for and believing in its worth.

Latimer had to deal with John Tallis immediately, and in such a way that no one afterward would look back on it with shame. Victor Narraway had been chosen to bear the burden of defending a man who was totally indefensible. He was strategically and emotionally trapped, exactly as if he were besieged in the city of his own duty, and there was no escape, no relief column coming.

It was already late. There was no point in waiting any longer. The situation would not get better. He turned away from the sheet of light on the river and walked into the shadows again, making his way back toward the barracks and the makeshift prison where John Tallis was being kept until his trial, and inevitable sentence of death.

He must begin tonight.

THE GUARDS STOOD TO ATTENTION OUTSIDE THE PRISON door. In the darkness it was hard to see their faces, so their expressions appeared blank. They looked at Narraway with indifference. One of them held up an oil lamp. They were both young, but they had been in India long enough for their fair skins to be burned dark by the sun. They recognized the insignia of rank on Narraway's uniform.

"Yes, sir?" the taller of the two said with no flicker of interest.

"Lieutenant Narraway, to see the prisoner," Narraway told him. He expected distaste, a forced civility. He saw nothing at all. Was the man genuinely impartial, or—after the siege—had he no feelings left?

"Yes, sir," the man said obediently. "You'll pardon me, but may I have your sidearm, sir? No weapons allowed when you're with the prisoner."

Narraway remembered with a chill that the prisoner who escaped had murdered the guard with the guard's own weapon. He handed over his revolver without demur.

A moment later he was inside the cell, standing face-to-face with John Tallis. The man was tall, a little hunched over; naturally lean, but it seemed the low rations and the exhaustion from first the long, burning summer under siege, and now imprisonment, had left him gaunt. He still wore his army uniform, but the trousers bagged on him. The tunic hung hollow over his chest and pulled a little crookedly at the shoulders. His thick, black hair was lank and his blue eyes startling against the sun-weathered skin of his face. He might have been any age, but Narraway knew he was thirty.

Narraway introduced himself. "I'm going to defend you at your trial," he explained. "I need to talk to you because I have no idea what to say. I know your regimental history because it's a matter of record. Everyone agrees you were one of the best medical orderlies they've ever known."

He saw Tallis lift his chin a little, his mouth twisting into a self-mocking smile. His teeth were white and perfect. "That'll come in useful if I'm ever charged with incompetence," he said, his voice cracking a little. "Unfortunately, it doesn't help now."

Narraway struggled for something to ask that might offer any mitigation. What on earth did Latimer think he could do? There was no defense! He was going to be completely useless.

"Tell me what happened," Narraway said aloud. "Exactly. Give me all the details you can remember. Go back as far as you need in order to make some sense of it."

Tallis looked incredulous. "Sense? When did you get here, yesterday? There isn't any sense. It's a colossal pileup of one idiocy after another. Bullets greased with pig fat, cow fat. It's probably bloody mutton anyway! Nobody's listening to anyone. People are just settling old scores, or shooting scared at anything that moves."

"You must have had some reason for helping Dhuleep," Narraway said desperately. "Give me something, anything at all to say on your behalf."

Tallis's eyes opened wider. A look of terror was naked in their blue depths for a moment; then he concealed it. He swallowed convulsively, his throat so tight he all but choked. "I didn't do it," he answered. "And I haven't any idea who did."

Narraway was at a total loss. Tallis was not justifying himself, not making excuses, not blaming anyone else. He was just giving a sheer, blank denial.

"But there was no one else who could have," Narraway said as calmly as he could manage. "Everyone else's whereabouts are accounted for, one way or another."

"Then someone is lying, or got it wrong," Tallis answered. "I did not kill Chuttur Singh or let Dhuleep Singh go. You have to prove that."

"I've got less than two days," Narraway protested. "Captain Busby's already been through all the details of the night, and Major Strafford. There was no one else who could've done it."

"I didn't do it," Tallis said simply. He gave a shrug of his bony shoulders. "I'm a medical orderly. I only kill people by accident, never on purpose."

Narraway was startled, angry; then suddenly he saw the black humor in Tallis's eyes. In that instant he felt a wave of compassion for the man's courage. In other circumstances, a thousand miles from here, he could have liked him. He licked his dry lips. "Where were you when Chuttur Singh was murdered?" he asked.

Tallis thought for a moment. "If it happened when they say it must have happened, I was in the storeroom, alone. I was counting what supplies we had, and going over what we could possibly get ahold of if any kind of relief supplies came in, and considering what we could make for ourselves with things from the bazaar," he replied. "If I could prove it, I would have already. It's a pretty good mess in there. We've been making do for a long time. I'm just about out of inventions."

"Did you not make lists of anything, inventory, notes about what to get?" Narraway struggled to think of something that could help support Tallis's claim.

"Certainly," Tallis replied, "but I can't prove when I wrote them. I could have done it anytime in the previous twenty-four hours. Believe me, I count those damn things in my sleep, hoping I've got it wrong and that we have more supplies left than I thought. I sometimes even get up in the night and count again, hoping items have got together and bred—like bedbugs."

Narraway ignored the analogy. "Did you know Chuttur Singh?" he asked.

Tallis looked away, and when he spoke, his voice was thick with emotion. "Yes. He was a good man. Silly sense of humor. Always coming up with crazy jokes that weren't funny. But he made me laugh, just because he laughed."

That sounded so normal to Narraway; it was absurd that they should now be talking about murder, thinking about an execution. It was a nightmare he must wake up from. He used to know how to do that, when he was a boy—make himself wake up. "And Dhuleep?" he asked.

"Different altogether," Tallis replied, watching Narraway closely. "Quiet. Never knew what he was thinking. He used to recite poetry to himself. At least I think it was poetry. It could have been a string of curses, or a recipe for curry, for all I know. Or a letter to his grandmother." He blinked. "If they hang me, will you write a letter to *my* grandmother? Tell her I died bravely? Even if I don't?"

Narraway drew in his breath to remonstrate with him, tell him not to be flippant or not to give up hope, but the words slipped through his mind and were all useless. They were going to hang Tallis in less than a week, get the whole matter dealt with and out of mind before Christmas, for everybody's sake—everybody except Tallis and his family back in England, proud of him.

"If it should prove necessary, and you give me an address, of course I will," he said instead, as if it were the natural answer. But it was also of no help at all.

Narraway knew Latimer was looking for more than Tallis's surrender. He needed some answers that allowed the men to have hope, which revealed a spark of sanity amid the senselessness and the fear.

"Somebody did kill the man, and you're the only one

unaccounted for," he pointed out sharply. "Everyone else was busy and in someone else's sight. Look, if you had a reason for killing him, if you know something about him, tell me." He started to say that for Tallis's own sake he should explain the circumstances, but stopped abruptly. Whatever Tallis said, it would make no difference at all when it came to his sentence, and they both knew it. If he pretended that wasn't the case, Tallis would think him a liar or a fool, and it would break the spiderweb-thin thread of connection between them.

He began again. "The regiment needs to know the truth. There's chaos and death everywhere. We need at least to believe in ourselves."

Tallis closed his bright blue eyes. "My God, you're young! What—nineteen? This time last year you were sitting for exams behind some neat, wooden school desk, waiting for the bell to ring and tell you time's up."

"Twenty," Narraway snapped, feeling the color burn up his face. "And I—" He stopped short, stung by shame at the absurdity of getting defensive about his age and experience. Tallis was facing trial for his life, and he had been offered nothing better than the most junior lieutenant to defend him.

Narraway lowered his voice and kept it steady. "Please, for the sake of the regiment, the men you know and who've trusted you—help them make sense of this. Give them a reason, whatever it was. Why did you want to rescue Dhuleep? What did you think he was going to do? If you didn't mean to betray the patrol, or get Chuttur killed, what went wrong? If someone is lying, who? And why?"

Tallis stared at him, started to speak, then stopped again.

"Are you protecting someone else?" Narraway asked sharply. "Is this some debt of honor you owe?"

Tallis was completely stunned. No denial in words could have carried such complete conviction as his silence.

"Debt of honor?" he finally said, incredulously; then he started to laugh, quietly but with a jarring, hysterical note underneath it.

Narraway felt ridiculous and painfully helpless. He had expected anger, despair, self-pity, but not this.

Then Tallis stopped laughing as suddenly as he had begun.

"I did not murder Chuttur Singh to pay a debt of

honor," he said quietly, almost mildly. "I'm a medical orderly who just happens to be wearing a soldier's uniform. I save lives—any lives. I'd treat a sick dog if I had one. Any debt of honor I owe is to medicine."

Narraway could think of nothing to say. He did not even know where to begin.

"For God's sake, man, think!" he said desperately. "Who was friendly with Dhuleep? Who might have owed him something, or sympathized with him? Is it possible someone had a . . . a debt to cancel, or a feud with anyone who was part of the patrol that was wiped out? If it wasn't you, then it has to have been someone else."

Tallis's brilliant blue eyes opened wide. "Is that why they're saying I did it? Because I owed someone, or hated someone on the patrol? I'm a medical orderly. I don't even know who was on the damn patrol! I'm one of the few men in the station who never has time to gamble or run up any debts. Half of our medical staff was killed in the siege."

"Then think of anything you've heard, gossip, tales," Narraway urged him. "We've no time."

"I've no time," Tallis corrected him. "The regiment

needs this incident put to bed as quickly as can be made to look decent. I can't blame them for that." He pulled his lips tight. "Happy Christmas, Lieutenant."

NARRAWAY SLEPT BADLY. SUCH DREAMS AS HE HAD WERE tangled and filled with a sense of hopelessness. He woke fighting against the sheets as if they were binding him, keeping him from escape. He was gasping for breath, in spite of the fact that there was nothing over his face. Again and again he saw Tallis's eyes. Was he innocent? Could this be a monstrous mistake? Did the authorities so desperately need to find the traitor, and make everyone believe justice had been done, that actual justice was the price? What other answer could there be? It seemed that no one else had had the opportunity to kill Chuttur Singh, so by default it had to have been Tallis. But what was his motive? What was Narraway missing that would make sense of it?

He was so tired, his head pounded and his eyes felt full of grit.

*H*E ROSE EARLY, WASHED, SHAVED, AND DRESSED BEFORE going to the mess and taking a brief breakfast. He liked the fruit they'd had in the summer—mangoes, bananas, and guavas—but there was none left now. He acknowledged other officers but sat alone so he could avoid conversation. He needed to think.

Latimer had given him one day to create some kind of defense for Tallis. An appeal for mercy was pointless. The only answer to a verdict of guilty was execution. Soldiers were killed all the time. Cawnpore was steeped in blood. Death was cheap. One more was barely even noticeable.

After he had eaten, he went outside and walked along the dusty roadway. The low bungalow houses of the officers were ramshackle now: three or four rooms set in extended areas that in better times would have been gardens. He did not hear the silent footsteps behind him and only became aware of Captain Busby when the man spoke, almost at his elbow.

"Morning, Lieutenant," Busby said briskly, not disguising the fact that he had obviously sought Narraway out intentionally. "Good idea to get away from the barracks a bit. Glad you thought of it."

"Good morning, sir," Narraway replied tersely, wondering what Busby wanted with him. He was not ready to discuss strategy yet, or accept any instruction, for that matter.

They came to a crossroads. Busby moved closer, obliging Narraway to accept the tacit guidance and turn along the wider road into the town.

The first building they passed was the library, looking dusty and deserted, its doors closed. There were two women standing on the steps with books in their hands, chatting to each other then glancing up the street toward the tearooms and the bazaar.

A couple of men came down from the breakfast club next to the library and nodded at the women, touching their hats courteously. They looked serious, avoiding anything more than the minimum acknowledgment of Busby and Narraway.

The billiard rooms were deserted this early in the day, as was the Freemasons Lodge with its handsome entrance. Narraway had intended to go toward the river.

He did not want to face the noise and the constant interruptions of the bazaar, with pleas to buy this or that, but Busby was intent on conversation and he could not escape.

"Doesn't look the same as it used to," Busby said ruefully as they passed the doors of the newsrooms. "Everyone's trying, of course, but the memories of the siege are all over the place, and the fear that it will happen again lingers. Every place you look at makes you think of someone who's gone. Thank God it's Christmas soon. Remind us who we are, what we believe in." Busby was talking casually, but his voice was edged with tension. He was a fraction taller than Narraway and perhaps seven or eight years older. His fair skin was burned red-brown by the Indian sun, and he walked with a very slight limp, as if from an old wound. There was a thin scar on the side of his left cheek, hardly noticeable.

"Yes, sir," Narraway agreed. "I've seen some of the children making garlands of colored paper," he added as they passed the theater, where in better times the younger men had performed all kinds of music and comedies for the general entertainment. It was silent now.

Busby smiled. "We must protect the men. They have

a right to expect that of us. We bring them here, thousands of miles away from everything they knew and loved, and expect their total loyalty. We receive it, and sometimes I think we take it too lightly. We owe it to them, especially the wives of those killed on the patrol, to see this trial to a swift end." He glanced at Narraway and then back at the rutted road they were walking along. "I hope you can see that." He said it with a lift in his voice, as if it were, at least in part, a question.

He outranked Narraway, but in the matter of the trial of John Tallis, rank should mean nothing.

"As rapidly as justice allows, sir," Narraway agreed.

"What witnesses do you propose to call?" Busby asked rather briskly.

"I don't know," Narraway admitted. "I only got the case yesterday evening, and I've never represented anyone on trial before."

"For heaven's sake, you're an officer, man!" Busby said dismissively. "I'm not a lawyer either. We're after the truth, not tricks of the law. A loyal Sikh officer has been cut to pieces, and ten of our own men were ambushed out there." He waved his arm in a general southerly direction. "Nine of them are dead. We've got widows, at least half a dozen more fatherless children. Tallis is responsible for that. The legality of it is just for the record's sake; don't harrow up everyone's emotions and open old wounds by asking a lot of unnecessary questions."

Narraway did not answer. There was no point in telling Busby that the colonel had asked him to do more than just tidy it away. Latimer wanted answers, wanted to understand what had gone so terribly wrong.

They walked a few paces in silence. A man pushing a cart of vegetables veered and jolted over a hole ahead of them. Two women—probably officers' wives, from the cut of their clothes—passed on the opposite side, inclining their heads slightly.

"I'm not sure if you are the right man for this," Busby went on, now staring straight ahead. "We might have been better off with someone who'd actually been through the siege and understood the suffering, the deeper issues."

"I think Colonel Latimer chose me precisely because I hadn't been through it," Narraway answered. "He wants this to be fair. If I'd been here through the siege, I'd have loyalties to certain men more than others, perhaps men to whom I owed my life. I might not favor them in any way, but people couldn't be sure of it, of my motivations."

Busby was quiet. They passed a small nondenominational church on the other side of the street. The post office was just ahead of them. They both looked battered, scarred by shells that had exploded too close. A shop nearby was darkened by the stains of an old fire, spreading out like the shadow of a hand.

"I don't know who you're going to call," Busby said suddenly. "No one else could have done it, you know. Don't go trying to raise doubt as to the honor of decent men. Apart from the fact that you won't get Tallis off—and by God, neither should you—you certainly won't do yourself any favors. If you want to make a career in the army, you'll understand loyalty." His voice took on a sudden, intense emotion. "That's what it's all about—courage under fire, steadfastness, and loyalty. You're no damn use to man or beast if your own men don't know that, come hell or high water, they can trust you."

He glanced sideways at Narraway, his eyes sharp. Then, after a moment's penetrating stare, he looked ahead again. "I assume you know that already, and I don't have to tell you? Make a good job of this and the whole regiment will respect you. Filthy responsibility, I know."

"Yes, sir," Narraway agreed, trying to put his words carefully. "My aim is to defend Tallis so that no one afterward—history, if you like—can say he wasn't dealt with fairly. I hope that won't take time, and I sincerely hope it won't necessitate my calling anyone as witness to an event that distresses them more than is unavoidable. But haste now may lead to grief; to dishonor that will later damage the regiment, and even the reputation of the Indian army in the future."

Busby stopped abruptly and swung around to face Narraway. "I think I underestimated you, Lieutenant. You're going to be a damn nuisance, aren't you? But if you think you can teach me the best way to handle this and earn the regiment's loyalty and respect, you are profoundly mistaken. Which I will soon show you."

"Yes, sir," Narraway said with a brief flicker of satisfaction. "I'm sure you will, sir, and with the utmost fairness. You can hardly fail to secure Tallis's conviction, considering the circumstances."

"I don't just want to secure his conviction, damn it,"

Busby said sharply. "I want to get the matter over with, with the least pain to the men and women who have suffered abominations you can't even begin to imagine." He swiveled around and started to walk swiftly back toward the barracks and the entrenchment where the army had been besieged. "Come!" he commanded.

Narraway turned and followed him, catching up with an effort. He did not want to go to the entrenchment again. He knew what had happened there, and could imagine the terror of it all. It was a barren square of ground, a hundred yards or so in either direction, with two- or three-story buildings along most of two sides. The rest was walled by simple earthworks, dug by spade and thrown up to less than the height of a man. During the eighteen days and nights of the incessant bombardment from Nana Sahib and his men, nine hundred people had lived there. Many had died of heatstroke, of cholera, or from their wounds.

Narraway still shuddered as he pictured the people huddled together, terrified, exhausted, trying to protect one another, waiting for relief that never came. He could see the ghosts of them in his mind. He wanted to turn and walk away, but he could not ignore Busby, who was his senior officer. And perhaps even more than that, he did not want Busby to know how deeply affected he was.

He stood silently. If Busby had anything to say, he would have to initiate the conversation himself.

In the distance a dog barked, a woman called out a child's name. There was an echo of laughter, exactly as if everything were perfectly normal—sounds of life, like new green shoots of trees coming up after a forest fire.

"Don't let them down, Narraway," Busby said at last. "You owe them."

Narraway wanted to say something brave, about justice having nothing to do with emotion or personal loyalties, but all the words that came to his mind sounded trite, and they would only anger Busby. Worse than that, he would not truly believe in them himself.

Busby was staring at him, waiting for his response.

"As I see it, sir," Narraway began awkwardly, "the most important thing is that when the mutiny's over and order is restored, India knows that British justice is fair and objective, sir."

Busby shook his head, momentarily taken aback. He started to speak and then changed his mind.

Narraway waited. He longed to leave this place, but he would not go until Busby did.

"I don't envy you," Busby said at last. "I suppose you have to make a show of it. Mind you do just enough."

"I didn't choose this, sir," Narraway answered.

"Nobody chooses their military duty, Lieutenant," Busby said tartly. He stared across the entrenchment. "These poor devils didn't choose to be here either. Just make as much of an effort as you have to so there's no question that the hanging is fair."

"Yes, sir," Narraway answered automatically. He was not sure if he meant it.

Busby turned and began to walk back the way they had come, his shoulders squared, but there was no spring in his step, no vigor.

Narraway waited a few moments longer, then left also, feeling as if he were turning his back on the ghosts, in a way denying them.

He needed to think. At the moment all he had for a defense was to try to discredit the witnesses Busby would call, and that was precisely what Busby had just warned him against. No one needed to tell him that attacking another man would earn him no friends. Most of them had already suffered deeply, lost friends and, in some cases, wives they loved, seen horrors Narraway himself could only imagine. He had been in India a year but he was an outsider to Cawnpore, and no one would forget that.

If his father had not insisted that the army would make a better man of him than a few years at university, Narraway would now be huddling beside a fire in some lodgings at Cambridge, worrying about cramming for an exam, and looking forward to going home for Christmas. His greatest discomfort would be trifling cold, the greatest danger not doing well enough and getting lower marks than he should have.

He had not chosen this. He remembered his last evening at home before taking the train to Southampton and then boarding the ship for what had seemed an endless journey south, around the Cape of Good Hope, into the Indian Ocean. Weeks cooped up, nothing more than a tiny dot on a measureless expanse of water, everywhere he looked nothing but blue. They could have been the only men alive on the earth and there'd be no way of knowing. Even the burning, blazing white stars in the sky above him changed, especially around the southern tip of Africa, before they started north again and re-crossed the equator.

That endless journey—for what? Some of the men he had come to know on that ship were already dead as a result of this savage mutiny—in so many cases, Indian against Indian. He had heard that there were only a little over twenty thousand Queen's troops in India and, of course, far more East India Company men, with all their wives and children—as opposed to Indians numbering uncounted millions.

Without realizing it, he was walking toward the river. Its swift, brown water was dangerous, full of snakes and other creatures, especially along the banks. But it still held a fascination for him: a sense of width and a freedom that the land did not.

Was that a log floating half-submerged in the water? Or a crocodile? If he watched to see, what else would he miss? Crocodiles sometimes came out onto the banks. He had seen their teeth, like a double row of jagged nails, needle-sharp. They could take a man's leg off in a single movement. He did not believe the stories that they were not aggressive and preferred to eat fish.

As he stared at the water, he wondered whether he was Tallis's best chance or his worst. There was only one possible end for Tallis, really— the gallows. The difference lay in whether it appeared that someone had fought for him, or not. Narraway himself was expendable. If everyone loathed him afterward and he went down in history as the man who had tried to excuse Tallis, that was the price of a swift and unquestioned execution, and the matter laid to rest before Christmas.

And if John Tallis was innocent? Was that even possible?

The log in the river moved and sank gracefully beneath the water, leaving a momentary wake behind it.

Crocodile.

The facts said that Tallis was the only one who could be guilty. And yet when Narraway pictured his face again, recalling it as vividly as if he had seen it just moments ago—the clear, burning blue eyes—doubts arose in his mind. Irrational, but undeniable, doubts.

Then who could be guilty? Who was lying? He could not imagine that several men were all lying to save the man who had really murdered Chuttur Singh and let

Dhuleep go. And if they were, would they allow Tallis to be executed for it?

Narraway could not get rid of the feeling that Tallis trusted him. All sorts of arguments came into his mind as to why it was not trust so much as hope, hope that Narraway could help. Or perhaps it was just a brilliant piece of acting. Or—and this was the easiest to understand—it was a denial to himself that he could have committed such a betrayal, a refusal to face the fact of his own guilt.

But looking at Tallis, that was not what Narraway had felt. He believed he had seen real desperation there, the kind a man has when truth is on his side.

How could Narraway even begin? If Tallis was innocent—and that was the only assumption he could work with—then either someone was intentionally lying, presumably in order to protect himself, or someone had been badly mistaken, gotten the facts wrong. Check everything—that was the only workable possibility, Narraway decided. It would at least provide him with his own set of details. Stand where each man said they had been, prove for himself that they had seen

41

what they said they had, time it all, go over the work they claimed to have been doing. Find the mistakes, the excuses, or the lies.

He turned and headed back through the trees toward the town.

The events of the mutiny were about a year old. It had begun in January, in Dum Dum. Almost every day since then there had been some new disaster, victory and then reversal, siege and relief, a new uprising somewhere else. How ridiculous to be trying one soldier for the death of one guard in the middle of Cawnpore while all over northern India, tens of thousands of men shot and slashed and stabbed one another.

He looked around at the officers' sprawling houses, with their verandas; their wide, scruffy gardens; the tamarind and mango trees, the lazy wind not stirring the leaves. In the summer the heat had been furnace-like, brutal. Now, at night, it was sometimes even cold.

He was not fighting with sword or rifle, although that would come soon enough. Scores of towns and cities were besieged or already fallen. This was only a respite.

In the meantime, as this day dwindled into nothing and disappeared, Narraway must prepare for the hopeless task of pretending to defend John Tallis, for which everyone would despise him, in spite of the fact that they knew he had no choice. He was cast as the second villain in a charade.

He increased his pace a little. He would speak with the witnesses Busby would be bound to call. That had to be the three men who answered the alarm and found Chuttur Singh dying on the floor in a pool of his own blood, and Dhuleep Singh gone.

He was walking past one of the rows of houses where various noncommissioned officers had their homes. They were all built of brick coated with white plaster, in various degrees of shabbiness. Verandas ran around three sides of each one, a flight of half a dozen or so steps leading up to the doors. They each stood separately in their own arid two or three acres, as if space was no object at all.

Narraway knew what they were like inside. The main door led into a wide, comfortless sitting room full of overused furniture—items that looked like they had been salvaged from a secondhand sale and intended only for temporary use, until something worthier could be found.

On either side would be smaller rooms, for beds, and one for a bath. The water for it, when needed, was left to cool outside in a row of large, porous red jars, so the officer's bath might be refreshing.

He looked back at the road and saw ahead of him a woman walking slowly. She had a small child in her arms and a large bundle of shopping carried in a string bag, its handles biting into her shoulder. She was bent under the weight of it and limping slightly, although from what he could see of her slender figure, she was not many years older than he.

Narraway increased his pace and caught up with her.

"Ma'am!" he said more loudly than he had meant to.

She halted and turned slowly. Her face was gaunt, and there were smudges of dirt where the child's dusty fingers had touched her cheek, but her skin was smooth, blemishless.

"Yes?" she said without curiosity. There was anxiety in her eyes, a shadow not unlike fear.

"May I carry the bag for you?" he asked. "I'm going

the same way you are. Please?" he added. He smiled at her. "My day has been fairly useless so far. I'd like to do something to make it better."

She smiled at him, suddenly and radiantly. It took away all the weariness and showed that she was indeed probably no more than thirty at the most, and pretty.

"Thank you, Lieutenant." She accepted, making a move to put the child down so she could unhook the bag and pass it to him, but he eased it off her shoulder and took it without her needing to. Its weight startled him. No wonder she had moved so slowly. The strings of the bag must have hurt her.

They started to walk again, still fairly slowly.

"You are new here," she observed, looking straight ahead of her. The child in her arms looked to be less than two, probably well able to walk, but not far or fast. It regarded him solemnly with long-lashed eyes of golden brown. Its hair was curly, and long enough for Narraway to be uncertain if it was a boy or a girl.

"Does it show so much?" he asked, referring to her observation of his newness. "Or do you know everybody?"

"I know most everybody," she replied. "Of course,

people come and go a lot, just at the moment." She made a sad little grimace. "But you look a bit paler, as if you weren't here during the heat." Then she blushed at her lack of tact in having made so personal an observation. "I'm sorry."

"No reason to apologize," he replied. "I never thought of that. I suppose I stick out like a row of sore thumbs."

She laughed at the image of such a thing. "Next time I see you in the parade ground, I shall think of a row of sore thumbs," she said cheerfully. "That will be a new insult for the sergeant major to think of. Except I see you're a lieutenant. I don't suppose you do a lot of marching around to orders."

"Not in the way you mean," he replied. "Although I feel rather a lot as if I'm marching round and round, to orders, and accomplishing nothing."

She looked at him curiously. "A lot of army life is like that. At least my husband always used to say so."

He heard the past tense in her speech and saw the moment of pain, the tightening of her arms around the child. There did not seem to be anything he could say that would help, so he walked beside her in silence for twenty or thirty yards. Then a hideous thought occurred to him. Had her husband been among the soldiers of the patrol that Dhuleep Singh's betrayal had killed? Suddenly, intensely, he realized that he could not afford to know the answer. He could not tell her who he was, and he was ashamed of that. It was a new and much harder bite into the soft flesh of his self-belief. How horribly lonely he was going to be after he had stood up to defend John Tallis, never mind that he had been ordered to do it, and that they could not hang Tallis until justice had been formally satisfied.

He had been trying to frame a few questions to ask her about Tallis, anything that might allow him to learn a little background. Now the words froze on his tongue. The strings of the bag were cutting into his hands. He wondered what was inside it. No doubt fruit, vegetables, rice, food for herself and the child. Would she marry again one day and have more children, or was this one going to grow up alone?

He wanted to speak with her. It seemed cold to walk side by side and say nothing, but consciousness of what the next couple of days would bring, and how differently she would see him, kept him silent. How long would it take him to live it down? The man who tried to defend

John Tallis. Is that who he would remain to the people here?

She stopped at a gateway outside a house exactly like all the others, at least from the outside.

"Thank you," she said with a shy smile. She bent and put the child down. It stood uncertainly on its feet before gaining its balance, then sat down suddenly.

"I'll carry the bag as far as the steps for you," Narraway replied. "Then you can carry him." He gestured toward the child, who was making an unsuccessful attempt to stand again.

"Her," she corrected him. "Thank you." She bent and picked the child up.

Narraway followed her up the path. They were still several yards short of the veranda steps when the front door burst open and a boy of about five came running out, a streamer of bright red paper in his hand.

"Mama!" he shouted with triumph. "I made three chains! All colors. And Helena made one too. It's not as good as mine, but I showed her how."

"That's wonderful." She smiled back at him. He had curly brown hair like hers but huge dark eyes that must have come from his father. "Helena?" she called out. "David said you made a chain too. Come and show me."

A girl of perhaps three stood inside the door, looking at Narraway warily.

"Come on!" her mother encouraged her.

Slowly she came across the veranda and took the steps, one down, standing on it, then the next down. She had a bright blue paper chain trailing behind her. She reached the bottom and joined her brother. She held the chain out to her mother, but her eyes were on Narraway all the time, curious but guarded.

He looked at the chain. "It's beautiful," he told her solemnly. "Did you really make it yourself?"

She nodded.

"Then you are very clever," he said.

Slowly, shyly, she smiled at him, showing white baby teeth.

"It's for Christmas," the boy explained. "To put up in the house."

"It will be lovely," he answered.

"Do you have Christmas?" Helena asked him.

" 'Course he does, silly!" Her brother shook his head

at her ignorance. "Everybody has Christmas!" He looked at Narraway. "She's only three. She doesn't know," he explained.

Helena held out the bright blue chain. "You can have it, if you like," she offered.

He drew in breath to refuse, politely, but saw the smile again, and the hope. He glanced momentarily at the woman, uncertain what to do.

"Take it." Her lips formed the words silently.

Narraway bent down a little to reach the chain and touched it. It was smooth and bright, the paper stuck together a trifle crookedly.

"Are you sure?" he asked. "It's very beautiful. Don't you want to keep it?"

She shook her head, still holding it out to him.

"Thank you very much indeed." He took it gently, in case she changed her mind at the last moment and clung on to it. "I shall put it up in my house, near where I sit, so I can see it all the time." She let it go and it fell loose in his hands.

The woman picked up the baby and carried her to the top of the veranda steps; Narraway handed the bag to her, then waited as they all went inside, the two older children still watching him as he turned and walked down the path again, holding the blue paper chain in his hand.

THE PRISON WHERE DHULEEP SINGH HAD BEEN HELD faced a large, open yard with buildings on three sides and an open dogleg way out, which was where most of the observation had taken place. Men had been working at various jobs of maintenance and repair, the sort of routine necessities that occupied most of a soldier's day when he was not in battle or marching from one place to another. They were tedious tasks but better than standing idle. It was easy to imagine leaving such a post, and then having to be a little imaginative with the truth in order to cover your absence.

Narraway stood in one place after another, checking the angles of sight, the possibilities of error or invention. Could any man have been so absorbed in his work as not to notice someone else pass by him? He did not believe it.

Had anyone left his stated position and then had to

cover his absence? It seemed like the only answer. Proving it would be almost impossible. Even the attempt to prove it would earn him enemies.

*H*e began his questioning with Grant. He had been the first man to reach the prison after Chuttur Singh had raised the alarm. He was not yet on duty now, having been on guard most of the night before. Narraway went to see him, feeling mildly guilty for waking the man when he must be tired. But lack of time left him no alternative.

Narraway went in through the gate, past some ponies picketed near a magnificent mango tree. He walked briskly to the veranda and up the steps, and knocked on the door. He knocked a second time, not really expecting an answer, then pushed it open and went in.

"Corporal Grant!" he called clearly.

There was silence.

Rather than call again, he crossed the sitting room. There was a large, rickety table in the center with a half bottle of brandy on it, four empty soda water bottles, and a corkscrew. Used glasses sat where four card players had obviously been the previous evening. There was also a box of cigars, a few odd magazines, a rather ornate inkstand, a bundle of letters, and a revolver.

The rest of the furniture he ignored, going past more chairs, a battered Japanese cabinet, and a corner stand with assorted hog spears, buggy whips, and a shotgun. He did glance at the various pictures hanging on the wall, hoping they might give him some idea as to Grant's origins and character. There was a school photograph. There was also a painting of a soldier with a woman in clothes of perhaps twenty or twenty-five years ago, judging from the style of the woman's hair and the line of as much of her dress as he could see. They were probably Grant's parents.

"Corporal Grant!" he called again, more loudly. He did not want to intrude into the bedroom. It would be ill-mannered. He would not appreciate a senior officer doing the same to him. Also he wished to make an ally of the man rather than an enemy, at least to begin with. "Corporal Grant!" he repeated.

There was a stirring from the room beyond, then the sound of feet on the floor and a rustle of fabric. A moment later Grant appeared in the doorway, tousle-haired, still half asleep. His trousers had been hastily pulled on, and his tunic was not yet fastened.

"Yes, sir. I am Grant," he said.

"Sorry to disturb you," Narraway began after introducing himself. "I wouldn't waken you now, except that I have only today to speak to everyone about the Tallis case. I've been detailed to defend him. Since you were the first on the scene, I thought I should begin with you."

Grant blinked. He was a good-looking young man, perhaps four or five years older than Narraway, with a slight country burr to his voice. Narraway placed his accent as Cambridgeshire, or a little farther north. His hair was brown with a touch of auburn, his skin burned by at least one Indian summer.

"Oh." Grant sighed. "I see. Well, I can't tell you anything more than what I've already told Captain Busby. Sorry."

"Finish dressing." Narraway made it more a suggestion than an order. "I'll make us tea."

Grant gestured toward the third room. "Kitchen's there. There are servants somewhere. Probably left me to sleep. I hate having them fussing around when I'm . . ." He did not bother to finish the sentence. Narraway already knew he had woken him.

Ten minutes later they sat in the central room with tea in front of them on the table. Grant was in full uniform and freshly shaved. But he still looked tired, and there were dark smudges around his eyes. He seemed nervous, but Narraway attributed that to the stress of remembering a shocking experience and having to recount it, knowing that it would end in the execution of a man he had possibly known quite well and certainly trusted.

"I don't know what I can tell you that makes any difference," Grant said.

"Just tell me what happened," Narraway replied. "If I know what you're going to say to Captain Busby, at least I have the chance to prepare for it."

Grant shook his head. "It won't make any difference," he said unhappily. "I don't know what the devil got into Tallis. I always thought he was a decent chap. In fact, I liked him. Everyone did. Well . . . one or two of the officers thought his sense of humor was a bit off." He looked at Narraway quickly. "They just didn't understand. When you deal with illness and injuries every day, if you don't laugh sometimes, even at crazy things, you go mad."

"You have been out here long?" Narraway asked, looking at Grant curiously, wondering what his experiences had been that caused him to speak with such feeling.

"Couple of years," Grant replied. "I was in the Crimea before that."

Narraway winced. The disasters of that war, the fatal mistakes, were legend already. "Balaklava?" he asked, before he thought of the possible inappropriateness of the question in the present circumstances.

Grant pulled a wry face. "Thank God for Colin Campbell," he said briefly.

Narraway was impressed, in spite of himself. "Were you there with him?"

Grant straightened in his seat a fraction, some of his weariness disappearing. That was an answer in itself. "Yes. Another damn stupid war we got into by accident because we didn't look where the hell we were going!" He rubbed his hand over his brow, pushing the heavy hair back. "Sorry. There are times when I'd put the whole damn government on horseback and order them to charge the enemy guns—with bullets coated in pig grease! Mixed metaphor. Sorry. I lost friends in that too."

Narraway sat silent, thinking of all the young men who had died needlessly because someone didn't know, or didn't think about, what they were doing. Every one of them had been somebody's son, somebody's friend.

Grant rubbed his hands over his face and drew in a long breath, letting it out in a sigh. "Perhaps Tallis did go mad, poor bastard. I hate this more than facing the enemy in the field. But I can only tell you what I know."

Narraway jerked himself back to the present.

"That's all I want," he said quietly. It seemed odd to be in this silent, rather shabby house, sitting over cups of tea, talking about betrayal and murder conversationally, but with hands that trembled and voices that every now and then rasped in the throat. "You heard the prison alarm," he prompted. "Where were you?"

"About a hundred yards away, in one of the outbuild-ings," Grant replied. "I was checking munitions stores. I dropped what I was doing and went outside—"

"Did you see anyone else?" Narraway interrupted.

"Not ahead of me, and I didn't look behind. It's sort of cluttered there . . . sheds, outhouses, that sort of thing. There was a pony and cart off to the left. I just noticed it out of the corner of my eye as I ran to the prison."

"Anybody else moving? Running?" Narraway asked.

"No. I must have been the nearest person."

"When you got to the prison block, the outside door was open?"

"No. It's a makeshift prison. The real prison was too badly shelled. This does pretty well because it was a magazine of some sort. Not hard to make a couple of cells inside, and the whole thing locks only from the out-side. Ideal, really. Escape-proof, without help."

"Any other prisoners there at the time?"

"None except Dhuleep." Grant looked down at his lean, sunburned hands on the table. "Before the mutiny there would be the occasional insubordination, drunken fights and things, maybe even a theft or two. Since the siege and the massacre, no one steps out of line. Those of us left are . . . close." He looked up, hoping Narraway would understand without the need for explanation.

Narraway nodded. "What had Dhuleep done?"

"Dereliction of duty. Off his guard post at night. I thought he'd just gone to get some sleep or something like that. We're all tired, a bit jumpy." He sighed. "But of course he could have been anywhere."

"Most likely trying to find information about the patrol," Narraway replied.

Grant looked down at the table again. "Yes—I suppose so. Looks like it now, doesn't it?"

"How did you get in?"

"It's easy enough from the outside. The key's there."

"What did you find when you entered?"

Grant's face tightened, his eyes suddenly bleak. "Chuttur Singh was on the floor in the main room outside, lying near the door. He must have used his last ounce of strength to reach up and pull the alarm. The cell door was open. There was no one inside, just Dhuleep's bedding on the floor and a plate of food, spilled . . . and blood. Lots of it. There was a trail of blood from the cell across the floor to where Chuttur had crawled. He was in a terrible state, his uniform slashed half to pieces, scarlet with his own blood. His face was gray, what I could see of it. He could hardly move." He stopped speaking for several seconds, emotion choking him at the memory.

Narraway waited.

A clock ticked on the mantelpiece. Somewhere outside a child shouted, its voice innocent, happy.

"He was dying," Grant went on with an effort. "He told me Dhuleep had escaped and to go after him. He had to be stopped because he knew about the route of the patrol. I wanted to stay and help him. He was . . . there was blood everywhere!"

He looked up at Narraway, agony in his face. "I should have stayed," he said hoarsely. "I left him and went after Dhuleep. I—I was desperate that he shouldn't get away, because of what Chuttur said about the patrol."

"How long had Dhuleep been in the cell?" Narraway asked.

"A day or two, I think," Grant replied.

"So they didn't know he had this information, or

they would have changed the patrol route, or time, or something?" Narraway said.

"Can't have," Grant agreed miserably. "But the patrol was ambushed. I know that for a fact."

"How?"

"Tierney told me."

"Tierney?"

"The one man from the patrol who lived, although he's in a bad way. He said they were taken totally by surprise and pretty well massacred. That's what letting Dhuleep go did. That's why they'll hang Tallis." His voice cracked. "God, it's a mess. Not that Tallis doesn't deserve it for what happened to poor Chuttur Singh. Regardless of what happened to the patrol, no one should die lying on the floor, alone. I shouldn't have left him." Grant stared into the distance, perhaps into a place inside his head rather than beyond the walls of the small, shabby house. "We didn't even get bloody Dhuleep anyway!"

"Did you find any trace of him?" Narraway asked, although he could not think what difference it would have made in the end.

"Not then. I suppose we thought we were on his heels and we'd catch up with him if we went fast enough. Damn lot of use that was." He sank into a silent misery, slumped in the chair, his tea ignored.

"So the others arrived soon after you? Attwood and Peterson?" Narraway continued.

"Yes."

"How long were you alone before they came?" Narraway asked.

Grant chewed on his lip. "About half a minute, maybe more, maybe less."

"Tell me what you did again, exactly."

"I went to Chuttur Singh." Grant was concentrating intensely, his mind back in those first awful moments. "I . . . I saw all the blood, and I knew he was fatally wounded. I just wanted to . . . I don't know. To say 'save him' is ridiculous. There was so much blood on his clothes, on the floor, it was clear he was beyond help. I suppose you don't think. You just . . ." He stopped. His face was ashen.

Narraway tried to keep the image from forming in his own mind, and failed. "You went to Chuttur Singh on the floor and realized he was past help. Then what?"

"He said . . . 'Dhuleep's gone,' I think. Something about someone else coming in, took him by surprise. Let Dhuleep out. He was mumbling, choking. I remember he said 'gone.' And then, 'Get him, he knows the patrol.' The man must have gone in the time it took Chuttur to crawl from the cell to the alarm." Grant was sweating, as if in his imagination he had made that desperate crawl himself.

"Then what?" Narraway asked.

"Then I looked into the cell, and he was right . . . of course. Dhuleep was gone. There was nothing there except blood and the heap of bedding, blood on that too. That was when Attwood and Peterson came."

"You told them what had happened?" Narraway pressed him.

"I told them that Dhuleep knew about the patrol and we had to catch him. Someone—I don't remember who—kneeled to see if he could help Chuttur, then we all went outside to hunt Dhuleep."

"Did you go together or split up?" Narraway was still clinging to the hope that one of them might have seen someone else.

Grant's voice took on a weariness. "We started within

sight of one another, but when there was no sign of him, we split up. I went west. I think Attwood went south and Peterson went down to the river, but I'm not sure."

"Did you draw others into the search? Ask people? Send anyone else out?" Narraway asked.

"Yes, of course. Anyone we spoke to."

"Did you find any sign of him?" Narraway went on. "What were you looking for anyway? Footprints? How would you recognize his? Anyone who'd seen him? Who else was around? Soldiers, women and children, civilians? Who could have seen him? Surely someone must've, with the knowledge of hindsight?"

"Of course," Grant agreed with a twisted smile. "With hindsight! A Sikh soldier in uniform. Not remarkable on any military station in northern India. No one knew that he was escaping. They probably didn't give him a second look."

"He'd just slashed a man to death," Narraway pointed out. "Those long, curved swords the Sikh soldiers carry are lethal! You said there was blood everywhere. Poor Chuttur bled to death. Dhuleep wouldn't have escaped without a mark on him. His trousers might have kept out of it, being draped and tight at the ankles as they are, and if they were dark or striped, you might not have noticed. But his tunic would be light, and they're loose and long-skirted." He waited expectantly, watching Grant's face.

"Perhaps he took it off?" Grant replied after a moment or two. "He'd have had to. You're right, there must have been blood on it. But he did get away, and it doesn't matter now. He'll be miles from here. God knows where. I certainly don't."

"You said you didn't find any trace of him then." Narraway was not ready to give up. "Did you later?"

"Yes." There was no light of satisfaction in Grant's face. "There was blood, just splashes here and there. And stains against a wall and a doorpost. Didn't help. I'd like to think some of it was his, but I don't know whether Chuttur even got a blow in or not."

He lowered his eyes, his mouth pulled tight. "I'm sorry. I liked Tallis. He seemed to be one of the best. But if he engineered Dhuleep's escape, then I'll be happy to see him hanged. I don't have to do anything but tell the truth for that. Someone came in from the outside. Had to. No other way. That person must have struck Chuttur, stunned him at least, and then let Dhuleep out, and maybe gone with him, leaving Chuttur to die."

"And you're sure you can't open that door except from the outside?" Narraway asked.

"Yes. Didn't I say that?" Grant bit his lip. "Chuttur couldn't even get out himself. All he could do was raise the alarm and wait, poor devil. You can't save Tallis, and you shouldn't." He faced Narraway squarely. There was sadness in his eyes but no doubt at all.

NARRAWAY FOUND ATTWOOD, THE SECOND SOLDIER TO arrive at the prison, working in the magazine. He had to ask his superior officer for permission to release him for as long as Narraway required him. It was given grudgingly, and Narraway and Attwood stood in the shadow of the magazine's huge walls to talk. Narraway could not help wondering why General Wheeler had not chosen this for his entrenchment, rather than the miserable earthworks.

Attwood was in his late twenties, a career soldier with a scar down one cheek and a finger missing on his left hand. He was short, solid, and barrel-chested, and had a vigorous Yorkshire accent. He regarded Narraway, who was from the south of England, with good-natured contempt.

"Nothing to help you, sir," he said briskly. "Heard the alarm. Ran to the prison. Got in behind Grant. Found the poor lad kneeling on the floor with Chuttur Singh, the prison guard. Damned good man. Best soldiers on earth, that lot, them and the Gurkhas."

"And Dhuleep Singh?" Narraway asked.

Attwood gave him a hard stare. "Gone, o' course. 'E's not going to hang around, once the door's open, is 'e? Look, I know you've got to put up some kind of a defense fer Tallis. It's the law, or we can't 'ang the bastard. But you're on a fool's errand. Not that we're short on fools around here," he added grimly.

Narraway's temper flared. "Anybody particular in mind, Sergeant?" he said sharply.

"Whichever damn fool put grease on the cartridges in Dum Dum, sir. Any idiot who'd served with Indians could've seen that one coming. Offend every last bleedin' one of 'em in one go!" He shook his head. "Don't tell me it was some genius who actually wanted this bleedin' chaos from Delhi to breakfast time!"

Narraway recalled what Grant had said about ignorance, but he could not afford to agree with Attwood, at least not openly.

"Fool's errand or not," he replied, "I have to do the best I can."

Attwood grinned, showing a broken front tooth. "Don't make a mess of it—sir," he said cheerfully. The "sir" was definitely ironic. "We don't want to have to do it all again, so as we can 'ang 'im with a clear conscience. Honor of the regiment that you fail nobly. Sir." In his own mind—and probably that of most soldiers'—his own three chevrons were worth more than the one pip on Narraway's shoulder. "But you'll fail, either way. No question to it," he added.

"Then help me to do it as nobly as possible," Narraway snapped. "When you were inside, what did you see, apart from Grant on the floor beside the dying guard?"

"No one else, sir," Attwood answered dutifully. "I

looked into the cell where Dhuleep had been. No one there, just bloodstained bedding on the floor."

"Lot of blood?"

"Quite a bit. As if there'd been a bit of a struggle, like someone—Dhuleep or Tallis—slashed at Chuttur, one man armed with one o' them long Sikh swords—edges like a razor, they 'ave—the other one trying to defend 'imself and not making much of it. Bloody murder, it was. Hardly a battle at all. Thank Tallis for that. Must 'ave caught Chuttur a hell of a whack before 'e ever let Dhuleep out. Damn coward, if you ask me—sir."

Narraway kept his temper with difficulty. It was not that he objected to what Attwood was saying, or to his contempt. He was angry with his own helplessness, and there was a degree of frustration inside him because he resented the fact that he had liked Tallis, that Tallis had even made him believe, for a moment, in the possibility of his innocence.

"Did you hear what Chuttur Singh said to Grant?" he asked aloud.

"No. Grant told us. Don't remember the words exact, but 'e said that someone 'ad come in an' caught Chuttur by surprise. Chuttur didn't tell 'im 'oo, of course. Maybe 'e didn't even see. Poor devil was dying when we got there. 'E'd been cut to bits." Attwood's face was bleak with anger and grief. He was a battle-seasoned soldier, but he was not immune to pain or the loss of a fellow soldier, even after the hundreds of deaths he had encountered and the whole brutal savagery of war.

"Couldn't 'elp 'im," he went on. "'e told Grant to go after the prisoner. Said 'e knew the patrol's route an' that we 'ad to get 'im. We didn't, but by God, we tried." He clamped his mouth shut and glared at Narraway out of tear-filled blue eyes, defying him to offer pity.

"Yes, Sergeant, I know that," Narraway agreed quietly. "Corporal Grant said you found traces of blood, and boot prints. Although I suppose the prints could have been anyone's. Nobody saw him, is that right?"

"Nobody that's saying so," Attwood agreed.

"He must have had blood on him," Narraway pointed out.

"To some people, one Sikh soldier looks like another," Attwood said drily. "And some folks are too scared, keeping their eyes shut to what they don't want to see. Everybody's frightened and sick and too tired to see where they're going half the time, never mind tell one

Sikh from another. Lost too many people, sir. Too many women and children. What kind o' people kill women an' children, I ask you?" He blinked, glaring at Narraway. "Don't you string this thing out, sir. We need to finish it. Get it all squared away before Christmas. Remember 'oo we are and why we're 'ere. Get me?"

"Yes, Sergeant, I do," Narraway answered him. "But it'll never be over if we don't do it properly."

"Then do it properly—sir," Attwood said abruptly. "Now, if you'll excuse me, I'll be getting back to my duty." He saluted and, without waiting for Narraway's permission, turned on his heel and marched back up toward the magazine.

Narraway found Peterson, the third man to arrive at the prison, sitting at ease under a tamarind tree. He was off duty for another hour or so and was smoking a cigar alone, staring into the distance. He was a private soldier of two or three years' experience. When Narraway stopped in front of him and asked his name, he scrambled to his feet and saluted.

"Sir," he said obediently, stubbing the cigar out with reluctance.

"At ease, Private Peterson," Narraway replied. "I don't think I'll take up much of your time." He looked at the dry grass the man had been sitting on and decided it looked comfortable enough. He sat down gingerly and waited until Peterson did also.

"Tell me about the escape of Dhuleep Singh," Narraway said.

Peterson looked at him with as much distaste as he dared show. "You the officer who's going to defend Tallis?"

"Someone has to," Narraway replied.

"You're new here, aren't you?" He added "sir" after a moment's hesitation. It was not outrightly rude, but bordering on it.

"I've been in India nearly a year," Narraway replied. "I've only been in Cawnpore for a couple of weeks. Why? Is there something I should know?"

Peterson kept his expression as bland as he could. "Thought so. You wouldn't defend Tallis if you'd been here any longer."

"Why not? Don't you think he should be tried?"

Peterson remained silent.

"You'd rather we just hang him and be done with it?" Narraway asked. "You're right, I haven't been here very long, not long enough to realize we'd sunk that far, anyway. Is there anybody else we should hang, while we're about it?"

Peterson flushed. "No, sir. I just meant . . . I don't know how you can defend the man, that's all. The whole patrol was wiped out—all but Tierney, and he'll likely not make it. That's all down to Tallis, because if Dhuleep hadn't escaped, that ambush wouldn't have happened. If they'd been attacked out in the open, it would've been a fair fight."

"There's nothing fair about war, Private Peterson. I thought you would have known that, after three years' experience. But trials are supposed to be fair. That's the whole point of them. Justice, not revenge. We're meant to be above hanging a man just because we think he might have done something we don't like."

Peterson swiveled around to face Narraway, his eyes blazing. "Something we don't like?" He all but choked on the words. "He let Dhuleep out to betray the patrol so they were butchered. And one of them slashed poor

Chuttur Singh to death. I think 'don't like' is a bit pale— sir!"

"Yes, it is," Narraway agreed. "And after we are satisfied that he is the one who is responsible for all of it, we'll hang him from the strongest branch and leave him there to swing. But after—not before."

"He's the only one who could have," Peterson responded. "Captain Busby questioned everyone. There's no one else it could be."

"Then we'll have no problem proving that at trial," Narraway said, surprised that he was still reluctant to give up hope that there was some other explanation. "Tell me what happened when you got to the prison after the alarm went off."

Peterson essentially repeated what Grant and Attwood had said. He chose slightly different words, more from his own vernacular, but the facts and emotions were the same. When he had finished, he kept his eyes fixed on the middle distance, where two young women were walking with children by their sides. Narraway thought of the woman he had met earlier, the children with their colored paper chains, Helena's smile.

"We need this finished," Peterson said quietly. He took a long breath and let it out slowly. He was not looking at Narraway, and yet he was very clearly speaking to him, his voice low and urgent. "Everything we thought we knew for certain has got blown away. People we trusted turned 'round and killed us, all over the place. But Christmas is Christmas, anywhere. We've got to remember who we are. What things are like at home. What we believe in, if you"—finally he turned and faced Narraway, meeting his eyes—"if you get what I mean, sir?"

"I get exactly what you mean, Private Peterson," Narraway said, with an upsurge of emotion that took him by surprise. Peterson had appeared so ordinary, even tongue-tied, and yet he had explained the heart of what was needed better than any of the officers. "I'll do the best I can." He said it as if it were an oath. Then he stood up, and Peterson scrambled to his feet to salute him.

$\mathcal{F}$INALLY, NARRAWAY WENT TO THE HOSPITAL TO SEE THE surgeon, Major Rawlins.

Perhaps the only point in speaking with Rawlins was to be aware of what Busby might draw from him, although Narraway knew there was little he himself could do with the information. He was going through the motions, because he had been ordered to. He wished he could forget Tallis's face, his eyes.

He went into the hospital building and walked along its almost-deserted corridors, passing a few orderlies, a couple of soldiers with bandaged wounds, one on crutches. He asked for Rawlins and was directed onward. The place smelled of blood, bodily waste, lye, and vinegar. His stomach clenched at it, and he wished he could hold his breath. How many men and women had bled to death here, or died of disease?

He found Rawlins busy stitching a surface wound in a man's leg. Narraway had to wait until the doctor had finished and could give his attention to the matter that, for him, was far from urgent.

He had a small office, where he invited Narraway to sit down, waving him toward a rickety chair. He perched on the end of a table himself. Rawlins was a little more than average height, broad-shouldered, perhaps in his forties. His fair hair showed streaks of gray only as the light caught it. His skin was deeply burned by many years in the Indian sun. He was a handsome man, far more obviously English-looking than Narraway himself. Narraway had heard that Rawlins had an Indian wife.

"Thought you'd be coming," the doctor observed. "But there's nothing I can say that'll help you. Wish there were. I liked Tallis. He was a bit of a clown at times, but a damn good orderly. Would have made a good doctor, given the chance. Saved a few men's lives with nerve and quick thinking." His face was suddenly sad. "Don't know what the devil happened to him. About the best thing you can do for him is not give him false hope. There's only one way it can end."

"He says he didn't do it," Narraway replied. "The facts say he must have, and yet I find myself hard put not to believe him. Or at least not to think that he believes himself. Why would he do it?"

Rawlins shrugged. "God knows. Why would anyone, unless they sided with the mutineers? But if you were on their side, why the hell would you stay here instead of slipping off to join them? Staying here, he had a good chance of being killed anyway. What a bloody mess. The last thing we need is to lose a really good medical orderly. Ask your questions. It's a waste of time, but I assume you have to go through the motions."

"I don't know what else to do," Narraway admitted. "There isn't any defense for such a thing." He wanted to tell Rawlins how helpless he felt and how totally confused he was by Tallis, but he despised complainers. "Busby's bound to ask you about Chuttur Singh. The way Grant describes it, Chuttur was struck on the head, probably dazed. Tallis let Dhuleep out of his cell. One of them took Chuttur's sword and hacked him to death, to try to prevent him from raising the alarm. Does that fit in with what you observed once Chuttur's body was brought to you?"

"Seems to," Rawlins replied, his face puckered with regret. "Based on the medical evidence, I can't see anything else possible, honestly. Chuttur had the exact injuries you describe. The Court will draw the obvious conclusion: Dhuleep was locked in his cell, so there had to be a third man, someone who got in from the outside. That person struck Chuttur, taking him by surprise or he'd have defended himself, and unlocked the cell so Dhuleep could escape."

"Any idea if Dhuleep was injured as well?" Narraway asked.

"Not a clue. I was told he left blood here and there, but not much," Rawlins answered. "Smudges, smears on a wall, a couple of footprints edged with blood. If he was hurt, if it wasn't just poor Chuttur's blood from his clothes, then he wasn't hurt badly. I'd like to think he was dead, lying out there in the scrub somewhere, or on one of those stony riverbeds, being picked apart by the carrion birds. But he was well enough to get as far as the rebels, because he told them where to ambush the patrol."

His face was tight with a sudden wave of emotion. If someone had brought the bodies back, Rawlins would have seen them, perhaps identified them before burial. And he would have treated the one man who came in alive but later died from his injuries—and also Tierney, the lone survivor. Being a soldier was easier, Narraway thought, than being an army surgeon. Even trying to defend Tallis was better than Rawlins's job.

"I don't suppose it matters anyway," he agreed. "As

you say, the facts allow for only one explanation. How is Tierney doing? Will he make it?"

"Could do," Rawlins replied. "Lost a leg. Wish I could have saved it, but it was shattered. You can see him if you want, but I doubt he can tell you anything. No question they were betrayed by Dhuleep, not that it makes any difference to your case either way. I wouldn't waste your time, and the Court's, even raising that question."

"I'd like to see him, if he's up to it." Narraway rose. "But I don't want to . . . upset him . . ."

Rawlins also stood. "He might be glad of someone to talk to. He's still in a bad way, just lying there alone most of the time. We do what we can for the pain, but he's not a fool. He knows everyone's clinging by our fingernails, as it were. We could all be dead in a few months if we don't turn this tide. The news is bad, isn't it?"

"Yes," Narraway confessed. "Far as I know. But we've got Campbell. He could turn the tide, by Christmas. Remember the Crimea, Balaklava?"

Rawlins grinned lopsidedly. "The Heavy Brigade: 'Here we stand, here we die.'" He paraphrased Campbell's famous exhortation to his men. "Not exactly what I had in mind."

"He won," Narraway pointed out.

"Yes, why shouldn't the tide turn?" Rawlins agreed. "I'll take you to see Tierney, if he's awake. This way."

Rawlins led Narraway into a small hospital ward where only one bed was occupied. A man lay slightly propped up on a pillow. His face was almost colorless and his cheeks were sunken, the bones sharp and protruding. His skin was stretched over them, papery and fragile. He might have been any age from twenty to forty. The bedding was draped over a frame above his right leg and the empty space where his left leg should have been.

Narraway wished immediately that he had not come, but it was too late to retreat. How did Rawlins deal with this sort of thing day after day and stay sane?

Although they had moved with very little sound, Tierney must have sensed their presence because he opened his eyes and looked at Rawlins.

"Hello, Doc. Come to see if I'm still here?" He gave a very faint smile.

Rawlins smiled back at him. "Only full-time patient I've got now. Have to see you," he replied cheerfully. "If I have nothing to do, they might not pay me. Then how will I buy a decent cigar?"

"That's what I'd really like," Tierney said huskily. "A decent cigar."

"I'll bring you one," Rawlins promised. "But if you set the bed on fire, then you can damn well lie on the floor."

Tierney laughed. It was a rough, croaking sound. "Like I'd know the difference! What've you got in this mattress? Sand?"

"Gunpowder," Rawlins replied. "So don't drop the ash, either." He gestured toward Narraway. "This is a brand-new lieutenant—at least, new to Cawnpore. Tell him about the place. We have decent mangoes here. And tamarinds, if you like them, or guavas. Nothing much else is worth anything."

"Any news?" Tierney asked, still looking at Rawlins.

"Nothing that I've heard," Rawlins replied. "If we win, I'll tell you, I promise. If we lose, you'll find out anyway." He gave a mock salute and left, walking back into the corridor, leaving Narraway alone by the bed.

Narraway lost his nerve to ask Tierney anything about the ambush of the patrol. It wouldn't make any difference to the trial anyway. It didn't matter where

Dhuleep Singh had gone or what he had told anyone. The murder of Chuttur Singh was enough to damn him.

"Where were you before here?" he asked conversationally.

"Delhi, God help me," Tierney answered with a downturned smile.

"I imagine it was pretty bad," Narraway sympathized.

"All so bloody unnecessary," Tierney replied, a trace of bitterness in his voice. "The Indian soldier's a damn good man. If we'd just listened, instead of always thinking we knew everything better. Took their loyalty for granted. Damn idiots should have seen it coming. Stupid bloody mess! You?"

"Calcutta," Narraway answered, thinking back to his arrival in India, confused, excited, and afraid, hearing rumors of unrest already. "Nearly a year ago. Glad I'd escaped the English winter!" He gave an ironic little laugh.

"Wouldn't mind a dusting of snow for Christmas," Tierney said. "Where are you from? You sound like Home Counties, but that could be education, I suppose.

I see you're a lieutenant, and you can't be more than twenty."

For no particular reason, except that he was eager to speak about something that had nothing whatsoever to do with India, mutiny, betrayal, wounds, blind stupidity, or trials, Narraway told Tierney about his home in the softly rolling hills and wide valleys of Kent. He spoke of long rides on horseback over the Weald in the early morning, with the light on the grass, which rippled like water in the wind.

"So what are you doing out here in the dust, eating yet another curry and wasting time waiting for something to happen?" Tierney asked with a slight, stiff shrug of his shoulders, his eyes smiling.

"Escaping boiled cabbage, gray skies, and biting wind with an edge of sleet in it," Narraway replied cheerfully. "And my father's wrath," he added.

"Which makes you much like the rest of us," Tierney commiserated. "Tell me more about Kent. Do you like the sea? I miss the sea, the smell of it and the cold, sharp spray on your face."

Narraway stayed and talked for close to half an hour, until he could see that Tierney was exhausted. Even then the soldier did not want Narraway to go. It was not until he unwittingly drifted off into a fitful sleep that Narraway walked softly away, grateful to have two feet to stand on, no longer even aware of the smells of blood and carbolic and other odors he would rather not name.

*H*E NEEDED TO BE ALONE TO THINK. HE WAS TOO FILLED with emotion. The futility of it all was overwhelming him. Everyone knew at least something of the needless waste of the Crimean War and questioned the purpose of it. The army that had beaten Napoleon at Waterloo had rested too long on its laurels. It was now cumbersome and sorely in need of updating.

The idiocy of the grease on the bullets, which had fired a whole nation's mutiny, was still being excused by some. But it could've been avoided so easily! Was there no communication, no Intelligence from which to foresee such errors and avoid them? Didn't the army speak to the government, or listen?

This was such a small part of the whole, and yet thinking of a few greased bullet cases, Narraway saw the enormity of even the smallest thoughtless act. One match could light the flames that consumed a nation, especially if the earth was already tinder dry—and no one had noticed that, either.

For everyone's sake, he must do the job that Latimer had commanded him to do. If he did not defend Tallis sufficiently well, if the Court could not say honestly that he had been properly represented, then Tallis's execution would in a sense also be murder. It would seem to others as if the regiment had convicted him in order to appear to have dealt with its own failure—vengeance rather than justice. They would look weak, not to be trusted; more than that, history would judge them to be without honor.

He continued walking, his feet making little sound on the earth and the thin winter grass. He passed walls broken by shellfire. They were crumbling away now. Ahead of him was a small, grassy mound with a few tangled bushes at the base of three trees. They were spindly, graceful. One was leafless and clearly dead. The other two still had rich evidence of life and in spring would no doubt have leaves, perhaps even blossoms.

A few yards beyond was a round stone-rimmed well. There was nothing there with which to draw water, no covering to keep falling leaves out, no rope or pulley, no bucket of any kind.

He stopped and looked at it curiously. There was an air of desolation about it.

"You can't want to stand here, sir."

He turned and saw Peterson a few feet away from him.

"Can't I?" He was curious. Peterson's face was white, his eyes hollow, without life. "Are you ill?" he asked suddenly. "You look—"

Peterson shivered. "That's the well, sir—that well. You don't want to stand here."

" 'That well'?" Narraway repeated.

"Bibighar. They massacred the women and cut them up, cut their heads off, and their . . ." He made a helpless gesture, half indicating breasts. "That's where they threw the bodies. Then their children after them. Scores of them, not all of them even dead. Filled it right up. You don't want to stand here, sir."

Narraway thought for a moment he was going to be

sick. His stomach clenched, and the outlines of the trees blurred in his vision. Sweat broke out on his skin. He turned to face Peterson.

"No," he agreed. "I didn't know it was . . . this well." Carefully and a little unsteadily he put one foot in front of the other and walked away, Peterson a yard or so behind him.

He had heard the story in whispered pieces, conversations that trailed away into silence. Cawnpore had been relieved on July 17, about five months ago now, but the ghosts of the siege were everywhere. The heat had been appalling, over 120 degrees in the shade. The horrified soldiers of the relief had found the corpses of more than four hundred men, women, and children.

In the Bibighar—the huge, two-roomed house in which Nana Sahib had kept the women of his pleasure during his occupation of the town—the soldiers had found the walls scarred low with the marks of sword cuts where women had been beheaded while on their knees. It was littered with hair and the combs that held it dressed, children's shoes, hats, bonnets, the torn pages of Bibles and prayer books. They had looked down to find their boots submerged in blood.

"I'd slit him open and pull his entrails out," Peterson said quietly, staring into the distance. "And burn them in front of him, still attached."

Narraway found his voice with difficulty. "Nobody would charge you for it," he said, coughing a little to clear his throat. "But if they did, I'd defend you. You wouldn't need any better skill than what I've got to get you off. I don't know how anybody here is still sane."

"Maybe we aren't," Peterson replied. "I wonder sometimes if I am. I wake up in the middle of the night and I can still smell it. Funny that, isn't it? I can't always see it, but I can smell it, and I can hear the flies. Do you believe in God?"

Narraway was about to answer automatically, but then he stopped. Peterson deserved better than that. Narraway himself needed more than a trite response.

"Well, I certainly believe in hell," he said slowly, selecting his words. "So I suppose I must believe in heaven, too. And if there's a heaven and a hell, then I think there must be a God. All this is unbearable if there isn't."

Peterson shook his head. "It's not the same as good and evil. Nobody doubts that. But is there anybody in control of it? I wonder sometimes if there isn't. If it all just happens, and that's all there is. Is there any sense, any justice? Or is it up to us to make sense and justice?"

"That's a hell of a question, Private Peterson. But I suppose Bibighar is as good a place as any to ask it."

Narraway thought for a while. It was also a place that demanded answers to such questions, not just for Peterson, or the Court that was set for tomorrow, or Tierney, or John Tallis. He needed them for himself.

Peterson waited.

"If there was somebody in control, you'd think they'd make a better job of it, I suppose," Narraway began. "What happened here seems beyond ordinary human evil. It's as if someone opened a door into . . . something else. But if hell were not more despicable than anything a sane man can imagine, then maybe heaven wouldn't be higher than even our most exquisite dreams."

Peterson shook his head slightly. "Wouldn't you accept heaven a little lower if hell could be . . . not this bad?"

"I don't think anybody asked me," Narraway replied seriously. "But if they had, I don't know what I would have said. After all, we haven't seen the heaven part of it—only this."

"But you believe in it?"

Narraway suddenly remembered the blue paper chain, and all the women who were going to celebrate Christmas, for their children. "Yes, I do," he answered. "Lots of people do, no matter what happens. We pick up the pieces and start again, for the sake of those who believe in us. If we can do it, then the best in us is trusting in something, reaching toward something. And that's what's important."

"Reaching toward God?" Peterson asked. "Sir?"

"I think so. Something that is as good as this is awful. Believe it, at least until you wake up dead and find it isn't true."

Peterson's face relaxed in a smile. "I didn't expect you to be so honest. Thanks. But I'd still leave this place, if I were you." He motioned to the well in the distance.

Narraway agreed, and with a brief salute he walked away from the Bibighar and its ghosts.

*K*NOWLEDGE, THAT WAS THE KEY. NARRAWAY SAT ON THE stone buttress of the old armory, now little more than a pile of rubble. The wind was rising, cold-edged, tossing the leaves on the trees. Information was what mattered, and how it fit together to form meaning. Everything was a matter of putting the pieces into the right order.

One of the difficulties was that you never knew if you had all the pieces or if something vital was still missing, something that formed the center of the picture.

What had he overlooked? Because so far, it all made no sense. He was a soldier, not a policeman, not a lawyer. But he should still be able to understand it if he tried hard enough. He knew the people, he knew the events. Did he know them in the wrong order? Was it something missing that was wrong, or one cornerstone point that was a lie? What one change would alter it all so it fit?

There had been no one inside the prison except Chuttur and Dhuleep. The door opened only from the outside. Grant had found it closed, had gone in and discovered the dying Chuttur, who told him that Dhuleep had escaped—that someone had engineered his escape—but he had not said who. Attwood and Peterson had then arrived, perhaps a minute later, and passed no one. Chuttur died without ever speaking again.

The three soldiers had gone looking for Dhuleep, but found only traces of his escape, signs of where he had been. The patrol had been ambushed and killed, all but Tierney.

The only man unaccounted for was Tallis. Tallis swore he was innocent. What was missing? Where was the lie?

It had to be Tallis—didn't it?

What was the information, the knowledge that Narraway did not have? He hated the chaos that had spread like madness across India, and the tiny piece of it that jumbled and boiled in his own mind, senselessly. He hated the internal darkness of it.

*H*E WAS ALLOWED IN TO SEE TALLIS WITHOUT QUESTION, although the guards' faces reflected a coldness, as if they imagined he was defending him because he wished to, not because he had been commanded. He hesitated, wanting to tell them how much it was against his will, then realized that would be childish. Half of what anybody did in the army was against their will. You still should do it to the best of your ability, and without complaining or trying to justify yourself. He was an officer; better than that was required of him. The fact that just over two years ago he had been a schoolboy was irrelevant. Many of these men had been soldiers in combat, shot at, acting with courage and loyalty at eighteen. Respect had to be earned.

He thanked them and went into Tallis's cell.

Tallis stood to attention. It hadn't been a day since Narraway had seen him, but he looked leaner, even grayer in the face. He was a man with only two or three days to live, and the shadow of that truth was stark in his eyes.

Time was too short for niceties. They stood because there was nothing in the cell to sit on, except the floor.

"At ease," Narraway said. Otherwise Tallis would be obliged to remain at attention. "I've spoken to the three men who answered the alarm and found Chuttur Singh. He didn't name you, but he said there was a man who came in and took him by surprise, and let Dhuleep out. And given the situation, that's the only answer that makes any sense. Dhuleep couldn't have opened the door from the inside himself."

"I know that," Tallis said quickly. "We all know there had to be someone else, but it wasn't me." His voice was level, but there was desperation in his eyes. "I was counting bandages and checking what medicines we had left in the storeroom. I can't prove it because no one else even knows what was there. I wouldn't have been counting them if I knew myself what was there! It's the only time I'm sorry we didn't have some poor devil sick, in need of medicine!"

"Ever treat Dhuleep?" Narraway asked. "Do you know anything about him?"

"I suppose I could always invent something," Tallis said with mock cheerfulness. "How about rabies? I let him go so he could infect the entire mutineer army. No good? I could say—"

"Tallis!" Narraway snapped. "I want to know if you knew the damn man. Did you ever treat him?"

Tallis looked slightly surprised. After a moment, he spoke seriously. "Yes. He had a bunion on his left foot. I'm intimate with it. I could draw you a picture. Couldn't cure it, of course. But I cured his indigestion. It doesn't exactly rate as a friendship. I cure people I don't like exactly the same as people I do. That's what medicine is about." He gave a sad, self-mocking smile. "Just like you defend people whether you think they're guilty or not . . ."

Narraway was temporarily robbed of words. He had not intended to be so transparent. "Give me anything to argue with," he begged. "What was Dhuleep like? Why did no one expect him to escape? Why was there only one guard? Who would want to help him? Who did he associate with? Who would want him free? If you didn't do it, then someone else did. For heaven's sake, man, help me!"

"Do you think I haven't lain awake trying to think?" Tallis asked. "Nobody likes a telltale, but I'd outdo the best actor on stage with stories that'd curl your hair if I knew any. I thought he might know something that was worth his freedom, but who would he sell it to? Latimer? Then I wondered if he was a double traitor, to us and then to the mutineers. Maybe he was let go on purpose, like a disease, to spread lies." He shrugged. "But as far as I know, he was just one more Sikh soldier who seemed to be loyal to us. Some are, some aren't. We can't afford to do without the loyal ones. I mean, look at it!" He swung his arm around, indicating the immeasurable land beyond the cell and the compound. "We're a handful of white men, a few tens of thousands, half the world away from home, trying to govern a whole bloody continent. We don't speak their languages, we don't understand their religion, we can't stand their bloody climate, and we have no immunity to their diseases. Yet here we are, and we expect to be liked for it! And we're all taken by surprise when they stick a knife into our backs. God help us, we're fools!"

"Don't say that in court tomorrow," Narraway said drily, although he was startled by how much he agreed with Tallis.

"Never let the truth spoil a good defense," Tallis said, paraphrasing with a crooked smile. "I haven't got a good defense, except that I didn't do it. And I haven't an idea in hell who did. I'm trusting you because I haven't *got* anything else. If you'd asked me a month ago if I believed in some kind of divine justice, or even in a man-made honor, I'd have laughed at you, probably made a bad joke." He shrugged his thin shoulders.

Suddenly his face was totally serious. The laughter had vanished; even the self-mockery was gone. "You see courage that's sublime. People enduring pain, disfigurement, losing parts of themselves so they'll never be whole again—and yet not complaining, still keeping the dignity that's inside them intact. People care for others, even when they know they're dying themselves. They keep faith even when it's idiotic, even when everything's gone and they know it's gone."

Narraway wanted to shout at him to stop, but he couldn't.

"I know they'll convict me, though I didn't do it," Tallis added, his eyes never leaving Narraway's. "But I still believe you'll find a way to prove that I didn't. Unfair, isn't it?" He grinned. It was a brilliant, shining smile, as if in spite of all that his brain told him, he had a kind of happiness he refused to let go of. He would not accept reality. "You should try being a doctor sometime. See this after every battle, every skirmish. They carry them in one after another, people who look to you to save them, and you can't, but you try anyway. One thing you learn, Lieutenant: You can't tell who's going to live and who isn't. You learn there's something bigger than you, bigger than anything sense tells you. I believe in the impossible, good and bad. I've seen lots of it. I did not kill Chuttur Singh, nor did I let Dhuleep go. I wasn't even there."

Narraway wanted to have an answer, something brave and wise to say. He wished, with a hunger that consumed him, to believe in the impossible, but he could not. So he did the only thing he could bear: He lied.

"Then I'll believe in miracles too," he said quietly. "And I'll find you yours."

He did not remain. He had already asked all the questions he could think of. He left the prison and walked outside into the dark. The vast night sky arched over him, brilliant with stars. The faint wind stirred through the branches of the few trees, a black latticework against the sheen of light. And he felt just as boxed in, as locked and shackled, as Tallis.

He walked for quite a distance. He knew that before he turned in he should report to Colonel Latimer, but he was putting it off as long as possible. He had learned nothing useful in the time he had been given to look into the case. Quite honestly, he did not believe any extension of the time would make a difference. It would just be putting off the inevitable and prolonging the misery for everyone, including Tallis himself.

He turned and went in the direction of the officers' mess, where he knew Latimer would be at this time in the evening. Probably Busby and Strafford would be with him, which would make it worse.

He passed a couple of small buildings and heard someone tapping nails into wood. He wondered what they were making. Household furniture? Mending a chair or a table? Or maybe working on a toy for a child, a Christmas present? A wagon with wheels that turned, perhaps? He could dimly remember one in his own childhood. Only fifteen years ago he had been the right age to play with such a thing.

Would the widow's little boy have a wagon, or colored bricks this Christmas? Perhaps Narraway could make sure that he did. He didn't have to give it to the boy himself; that might only embarrass her, make her feel obligated to him, and he did not want that. Would the boy even like a wagon? Wasn't it worth trying? The little girl, Helena, had given him the blue paper chain, certain that he would like it because she liked it. He should find something for her too. He would have to ask somebody. A woman would know.

He stopped and knocked on the door of the building where the banging came from. After several moments, a man in a leather apron came to the door. "Yes, sir?" he said politely. He was Indian, dark-skinned, black-haired.

"Are you a carpenter?" Narraway asked.

"No, I just mend things here and there. If you have a chair that is broken, perhaps I can help?"

"Actually . . . what I want is a small wooden wagon . . . for a child," Narraway replied, feeling foolish.

The man looked surprised. "You have a son? You want something for him for a gift, sir?"

"No . . . and yes. He's not my son, but he's lost his father. I just thought . . ." He trailed off, his confidence draining away.

"I can do that," the man said quietly. "I will make you one. Come back in a few days. I have many small pieces of wood. And red paint. It will not cost much."

"Thank you," Narraway replied. "I'd like that very much. My name's Lieutenant Narraway. I'll be back."

As he walked past the next open door he heard a woman inside, singing. Her voice was soft and filled with music. He had no idea who she was, but she was singing to someone she loved, of that he was certain. Probably it was a child. Reluctantly he moved on, out of earshot, toward the officers' mess.

At first Narraway was almost relieved not to see Latimer, and he had half turned to go when he noticed Strafford in a corner, and then Latimer beside him. He pulled his tunic a little straighter and squared his shoulders, then walked across the floor, threading between the tables and chairs and rickety stools, until he stood to attention in front of Latimer.

"Sir."

Latimer turned toward him as if he had been expecting this moment, and not looking forward to it any more than Narraway himself.

"Are you ready, Lieutenant?" he asked. His face was pale and tired. He nursed a glass of whisky in his hand as if it could feel his touch, his fingers caressing it.

"Yes, sir," Narraway replied. They both knew it was a lie, but it was the answer expected of him.

"You've spoken with Tallis?" Latimer pursued.

"Yes, sir."

"Any help?"

"Not much."

Latimer smiled; for a moment it softened the lines in his face. "Like him?"

Narraway was not prepared for the question. "Ah . . . yes, sir. I couldn't help it. Would have preferred not to."

"If you'd said 'no,' I wouldn't have believed you." Latimer sighed. "One thing you'll have to learn if you're going to make it in the army, Narraway. Know when to lie to your superiors and when not to. Sometimes we know the truth, but we don't want to hear it."

"Sorry, sir. I didn't know this was one of those moments."

"It wasn't. Your judgment is quite right. He's a likeable man. We need the kind of humor he brings, and the unreason, the ability to hope when it makes no sense. I wish to hell it had been anybody else but him. You can't save him, but for God's sake, make it look as if you're trying."

"Yes, sir." Narraway fell silent. He felt stupid, but there was nothing else to add.

"Busby'll give you a hard time. Expect it, and don't lose your temper, no matter what he says. He lost a life-long friend in that ambush. He'd served with Tierney a long time too. That's the fellow who lost a leg."

"Yes, sir, I know. I spoke to him. A good man," Narraway replied.

"Did you?" Latimer looked slightly surprised. "Tell you anything useful?"

"No, sir. Just thought I should speak to him."

"Well, you'd better go and get a decent night's sleep— or as decent as you can."

"Yes, sir. Good night, sir."

Latimer lifted a hand in a slight salute. "Good night, Lieutenant Narraway." Then: "Did you make any sense of it yet?" he asked suddenly.

Narraway felt the coldness deep inside him. "No, sir, but I will."

"That was the lie I wanted to hear," Latimer said with a faint smile.

NARRAWAY COULD NOT SLEEP. HE LAY ON HIS COT. IT WAS comfortable enough, better than many places where he had slept perfectly well over the last year, but restfulness eluded him. He turned one way, then the other, sometimes with his eyes closed, sometimes staring up at the ceiling, which was pale from the starlight through the window. Tallis's face came back to his mind, regardless of all his efforts to banish it away. This was an inescapable burden, suffocating him.

It was not only Narraway's career at stake, it was the whole regiment's honor, its belief in justice as an abstract, a perfect and beautiful thing that every man strove for. Except that that was nonsense. Some men strove for it. Many merely used the word as an excuse.

Narraway had not been among the soldiers who had relieved Cawnpore after the siege. He had been farther north. But he had heard about it. What the soldiers arriving had seen had driven them almost out of their senses. The vengeance had been appalling. No one had bothered with justice then.

Had he not seen the emotion in the men, the stunned look in their eyes, the sudden clumsiness in movement, as if they lacked coordination? The horror and the grief were too enormous to recover from in just a few short months. Maybe those men would never again be quite the same men as they had been before.

Right now, faced with the immediate decision of what to say at the trial in a matter of hours, Narraway dared not think about his future, but that time would come. He could not win; it was only the measure of his loss that counted. Some would judge him for trying at all, even though the soldier in them would know he was obeying an order he could not refuse. Reason would defend him, but emotion would not.

Again and again, he came back to reason. He could see very easily why Latimer needed to understand. It was not simply a matter of morale. Without understanding, they would commit the same errors over and over again in the future. For all he knew, they might be committing them right now.

What was he misreading? Was there something in the puzzle that did not belong? He must have some plan before morning.

He went over it again in his mind and came up with the same answers. There was no one it could have been, except Tallis. Tallis had sworn his innocence. And no one, not even Busby, could come up with a *reason why* Tallis should have wanted Dhuleep to escape.

Reason—that was the missing piece.

He could not think of anything that would justify letting Dhuleep escape. His hunger to see sense was growing more powerful, the need for an overall intelligence that promised future control.

He could hear no sound in the night air except his own breathing and the whine of an insect somewhere.

Then a thought struck him. Perhaps the act made no sense because it was not the result Tallis had intended. What if he'd wanted something quite different? Might he have known that Dhuleep had information about the patrol, and intended to kill him because of it? The original charge against Dhuleep was not serious, so in a few days he might well have been let go anyway. Maybe Tallis hadn't wanted to risk that? And the plan had just gone wrong when he reached the cell?

But how would Tallis have known Dhuleep had such information? And why not plan to kill him in some more discreet way—medically, to make it look more or less like a natural death—instead of just barging into the cell?

Or might Chuttur secretly have been a traitor as well? These days, nobody knew who was on which side. People crossed from one to another. After all, it was a mutiny, not a war with clearly defined lines. So maybe *Tallis* had been the one to kill Chuttur, but Dhuleep had managed to get away in the process.

But why would Tallis not mention such things if they were true? Was someone else involved, someone else he could not betray? Were there further traitors he must not warn? Narraway could not forget that Tallis had said he trusted him. Would he spend the rest of his life measuring himself against this one failure? Would he even have the courage to fight his hardest for Tallis, knowing he could only lose? And when it was all over, would he have the courage to watch the hanging, knowing that he had been the one hope Tallis had had?

Why the hell did Tallis not trust him with the entire truth, and yet believe he would still help, pull off some kind of miracle? They did not even know each other. Narraway had never represented anyone at trial before; he had no reputation for such a thing.

Maybe it was not Narraway that Tallis trusted, but British law? Then where the devil did he grow up, that he did not know there were miscarriages of justice at home as well?

A trust in the British? After the atrocities on both

sides of the mutiny, that would be absurd. And Tallis had surely seen the worst of all that. He was a medical orderly—no one could tell him about a horror that he had not already seen.

Narraway turned over again and pulled the blanket after him. He was cold and tired, and his head was pounding, but he was no nearer sleep.

Perhaps it was God Tallis believed in. That did not require reason. When circumstances were extreme enough, sometimes that was all there was to believe in. Tallis was a young man. He had chosen a noble path in life: healing others, even when it meant risking his own life. If he had stayed in Britain he could have been comfortable, respected, and safe. So maybe he had a right to expect something of God?

Was that the way he saw it? God would help him?

Why? God had not helped the thousands who had been murdered in the mutiny. He had not saved the women and children at the Bibighar well.

He turned over to the other side, then on to his back, eyes open, watching the starlight on the ceiling.

What did he believe in himself? What did he trust? That called for a harsh review. He had been brought up to attend church. Most of the men here had. Did he believe in its teachings, its doctrine? Did he even believe in the God the church taught?

He realized with a sudden chill, as if someone had snatched his blanket away, that he had never really looked far enough into himself to know what he believed. If he had to answer now, tonight, staring at the starlight on the ceiling of his bedroom in this battered and rather shabby house, did he believe in God?

He certainly did not *disbelieve*. But he did not believe in the grand and rather distant God of the churches he had been to. If He was a God for everyone, then He must be equally so for the Indian, or the Chinaman, or the African.

And yes, that God he did believe in. Maybe it was because he needed to. For everything on earth to be pointless, accidental, and without love or purpose was a sterility he would not entertain. It left no room for true laughter, beauty, or even love. It did not allow for hope, for that in man that forgives, nor for that in woman that nurtures endlessly, that will sacrifice to save her children without ever thinking of the cost.

For what did he trust God, the good parent?

Mercy? Perhaps at Judgment Day, if such existed, but there was scant evidence of it now.

Justice? There was scant evidence of that, either. But then, if there were, if good were rewarded with good and evil with evil, would either of them really exist? Would there be anything more than enlightened self-interest? No true virtue, simply a system of barter?

That was a world so ugly, so barren and eventually hideous, that he thrust away the idea. It was a kind of universal death.

No justice, then; except what man himself strove to make.

No biblical promise that he could recall had ever said that justice would come without pain or loss: simply that in the end, it would be worth it.

Faith? Certainly. But blind faith that did not expect immediate reward, a trust that did not look to be vindicated and explained at every step along the way? Was that what he believed?

Yes, perhaps it was.

Could he live up to it? That remained to be seen.

But a plan was beginning to form in his mind, a way to discover the missing pieces that would make sense of both Tallis's act then and his silence now. The truth must lie in the characters of Dhuleep and Chuttur themselves; something Tallis knew of them and Latimer did not.

Gradually he drifted into an uneasy sleep, filled with nightmares that ballooned and faded, sometimes acutely sharp.

*T*HE TRIAL OF JOHN TALLIS BEGAN THE FOLLOWING MORNing. Only the necessary attendees were present. Latimer had wanted as little attention brought to the details as possible. He sat at the top table with two officers Narraway did not know. Busby was at a small table on one side of the room with his papers spread in front of him, and Narraway was at the other.

Tallis, in uniform rather than his medical working clothes, sat beside Narraway. They had no suitable handcuffs or chains in which to keep him, but there were armed soldiers at the door, and in the room beyond where various witnesses were waiting. A couple of junior officers appeared to be ushers, and a third sat at a small table off to one side, pen poised to record what was said. How on earth he would keep up with the conversation, Narraway had no idea.

As soon as the formalities were dealt with, Busby began by calling his first witness. It was clear even from the brisk way in which he spoke, from the neatness of his uniform and the immaculate way his hair was brushed, that he intended to observe the letter of the law.

Of course, he knew he was going to win. There was no battle, only the pretense of one.

Grant was called. He came in straight-backed but looking curiously tired. He faced Busby, waiting.

Busby stood, speaking quietly, as if there were only the two of them in the room.

"I'm sorry to have to take you through all this again, Corporal Grant," he said gently. "I'm sure you understand the necessity. We must do justice here, not only to the dead and their families, but also to the living. It must also be seen by others, far beyond this regiment, or Cawnpore itself, that murder will be punished, fairly and justly, and that our actions are not taken out of revenge."

"Yes, sir," Grant responded, straightening his shoulders a little more.

Step by step, Busby led him through the events of the night in question: hearing the alarm, dropping what he was doing, and running toward the prison. He had him describe exactly what he did, what he saw, never dwelling on unnecessary horrors to give Narraway a chance to object that he was playing on emotions rather than facts.

"Thank you," Busby said when Grant had come to the end of his description. "Please wait there in case Lieutenant Narraway has anything to ask you."

Narraway stood up slowly. He was disgusted to find that he was shaking. It was absurd. He was going to lose. The battle was over before it began.

He cleared his throat. "Corporal Grant, when I spoke to you yesterday, asking you about this tragedy, you told me that Chuttur Singh was fatally wounded when you found him."

"Yes, sir," Grant said too quickly. He also was nervous, his body tight under the fabric of his uniform, his shoulders high and rigid. He had liked both Chuttur Singh and Tallis. This was clearly painful for him.

"We appreciate that there was nothing you could do for him, Corporal," Narraway said as gently as he could. "You said to Captain Busby that Chuttur Singh told you the prisoner had escaped and that recapturing him was more important than anything else, is that correct?"

Busby moved impatiently.

Latimer held up his hand to silence him.

"Yes, sir," Grant agreed.

"He told you to leave him and pursue the prisoner, Dhuleep Singh?" Narraway persisted. "Because he knew the route and times of the patrol?"

"Yes, sir."

"Do you know how he knew that?"

Grant looked slightly surprised. "No, sir."

"Yet you did not question it?"

"No, sir."

"You told me that Chuttur had said someone had come into the prison from outside and attacked him. I asked you if Chuttur Singh had told you who the other man was, and you told me he had not. Is that correct?"

Grant let his breath go slowly. "Yes, sir. That is correct. I . . . I don't think he knew."

"It isn't that he told you, and for some reason or other you are concealing it?" Narraway pressed.

Busby rose to his feet. "Colonel Latimer, this is—"

Latimer held up his hand. "Perfectly fair, Captain. Thank you, Lieutenant Narraway. We have established that Chuttur Singh did not tell Corporal Grant who attacked him, and we may safely presume it was because he did not know. Have you anything further, Lieutenant, perhaps regarding Dhuleep Singh's knowledge of the patrol?"

"Not at this time, thank you, sir." Narraway sat down with relief washing over him, his knees feeling like water.

Busby then called Attwood, who said much the same as Grant had. However, his words were not so identical as to make it seem as if they had conferred. Narraway could think of nothing to contest, and he did not want to risk making a mistake that could cost him credibility.

Finally Busby called Peterson, who added nothing of value, except in his careful and clearly honest description of how he had left the prison block and gone searching for Dhuleep Singh. It was he who had found faint traces of blood showing the path of escape. Busby obtained all the details from him, making the scene seem real and urgent, terribly familiar to those listening. It was Peterson who had gone in the direction of the Bibighar Gardens and the well.

"Did you search the Bibighar building for this man?" Busby asked.

Peterson was white-faced. "Yes, sir. He wasn't there." He was shaking very slightly.

"You looked inside the house?" Busby persisted. "You didn't avoid it . . . because . . ."

Narraway knew what Busby was doing, and he could not bear it. He stood up, facing Colonel Latimer.

"Sir, Captain Busby is suggesting that Private Peterson failed in his duty because of the horror of what happened there, and possibly out of his own personal grief. Private Peterson has told the Court that he looked. He is an honorable man and a good soldier. He is not charged with anything, and should not have his courage or his honesty brought into question here."

There was a murmur of approval from the man to Latimer's right, and both the men acting as ushers nodded.

"Thank you." Latimer nodded at Narraway. "Captain Busby, we are satisfied that Private Peterson has answered your question. No one found Dhuleep Singh, as is only too evident to all of us. If you have nothing further to ask him, then when Lieutenant Narraway has spoken, we will adjourn for luncheon."

Busby sat down, his face faintly flushed.

"Thank you, sir," Narraway acknowledged. "I think what happened after the alarm was sounded is very clear. I have nothing useful to ask Private Peterson."

Latimer nodded, his face expressionless.

"We are adjourned until two o'clock," he told them.

Narraway left alone, not that he was offered much choice. As he walked away across the open space, the cold wind striking him through his uniform, he felt something of a panic. No one openly snubbed him, but neither did anyone speak to him. In a way he was grateful. He needed time alone in which to think. The answer did not lie with any of the soldiers questioned this morning. He was becoming more and more convinced that it had to do with Dhuleep and Chuttur, and the information about the patrol. If only he could grasp the missing fact that would make sense of it. How did Dhuleep know? Was Chuttur involved after all? Was it Chuttur who knew, and was tortured for it?

That answer did not help Tallis's case at all though. He was still missing the key!

In the officers' mess he found a place in a far corner and sat eating absentmindedly. He had no hunger, but he knew that if he ate nothing he would regret it later. How could something as rich as a curry seem tasteless?

He left the plate half-finished and went to look for the sergeant who had spent the most time with the Sikh troops, Gholab Singh. He found him in a small office in one of the barracks still largely intact.

"Yes, sir?" Gholab Singh said courteously, rising to his feet.

Narraway introduced himself and told the sergeant to be at ease.

"What can you tell me about Dhuleep Singh?" he asked as soon as the man was seated again. "Other than what I have read in his army record."

Gholab looked uncomfortable. "I am ashamed for him, sir," he said quietly. "To rebel openly I cannot fault him for, at least not greatly. But to betray behind the back is another thing, altogether different. He was a sneaky bastard, sir. Very clever. Always listening and adding up in his mind, that one."

"It doesn't surprise you that he knew the times and routes of the patrol?" Narraway asked.

Gholab shook his head sadly. "He was a tricky one. He darkens all our names."

"And Chuttur Singh?" Narraway asked.

"A good man," Gholab said without hesitation. "I know his brother and his cousin. Good men, all of them. Maybe a bit too trusting. Not a bad fault in a man. Better than deceit." He shook his head. "Cousin to a snake, Dhuleep. May he eat the dust."

Narraway stayed a little longer, asking questions as they came to his mind, but Gholab could tell him nothing further. He had no idea if either Chuttur or Dhuleep had any personal acquaintance with Tallis.

THE AFTERNOON BEGAN WITH BUSBY CALLING RAWLINS. The room sat in total silence. Tallis stared white-faced into the distance as the surgeon described the injuries to Chuttur Singh.

Busby's expression was one of shock and deep grief. No one could imagine it. Each man in the room had seen the injuries of war, seen soldiers cut down beside them, friends, people with whom they had shared jokes and food, and dreams of home. This was different. Civilized men fought for their ideals, for their countries, sometimes whether they believed them right or wrong. To betray a man who had trusted you was an act that deserved no mercy. Indeed, if the law was to stand for anything, if it was even to survive, such an act must be punished. And Tallis knew that.

"Did Chuttur Singh fight back, Major Rawlins?" Busby asked.

"There were deep slashes on his arms, which suggest he may have tried to defend himself," Rawlins replied. "And I believe there was a degree of blood on his own sword. I can't tell you what that means because his sword may have been used against him."

"To sum up," Busby said grimly, "There was a blow to the back of his head, hard enough to have stunned him, after which he was hacked to death with at least fifteen violent blows from a sword, most likely his own."

"Yes," Rawlins said with a catch in his voice.

"He bled to death?" Busby pressed.

"Yes."

"Have you ever seen wounds like this before?" Busby continued.

Rawlins looked, if anything, even paler. "Of course I have," his voice grated. "I was with the regiment that relieved Cawnpore after the siege. I stood almost ankle-deep in blood at the Bibighar, where the women and children were hacked to pieces. Some of them were the families of my friends. I refuse to describe it for you. Those who saw it will never forget, and those who did not can look at the faces of those who did and thank God for their escape."

Busby looked at him with surprise, then glanced around at the other men in the room. Narraway followed his eyes and saw what he must also have seen. Every other man there had, at one time or another, received help from Rawlins. He had relieved their pain, sat with them through times of agony that could not be helped, comforted them when they feared maiming or death, mourned with them over loss. Busby would be a fool to challenge him.

"And the men of the patrol that was ambushed," he said, changing his line of approach. "Did you see their bodies when they were brought home . . . those that were?"

"They were buried where they fell," Rawlins replied. "The two who were alive—yes, I saw them. One died shortly after being brought back. The other looks as if he will recover, but he has lost the greater part of one leg."

"The dead, they too were hacked to pieces," Busby said, making it a conclusion rather than a question.

"They were ambushed and died in battle," Rawlins snapped. "You have no business, sir, to suggest that they did not fight back."

Busby retreated. "I apologize. I did not mean to imply such a thing at all. They were surprised, betrayed, but I imagine they took a good few of the enemy with them—unlike poor Chuttur Singh, who was betrayed in quite a different manner, and outnumbered two to one."

Rawlins said nothing.

Busby moved only slightly. The room was small, and there was no space to spare.

"Is there anything else that you can tell us of this terrible event that might help us bring the matter to resolution and allow justice to be done?"

Rawlins leaned forward a little, staring at Busby.

"Captain, it is not my job to judge any man, only to heal him if I can. I do not know exactly what happened in that prison, who did it, or why. I have told you what the injuries were to Chuttur Singh, who I examined after he was brought to the medical wing. I cannot deduce anything more than I have already told you."

"Thank you, Major Rawlins. I had assumed as much." Busby seemed about to add something further, then changed his mind and turned to Narraway. His expression was bland, polite even, except for a bright spark of anger in his eyes.

Narraway rose to his feet, knowing this was his last chance. He still had a small, gnawing pain inside him that he could not ignore. What if Tallis was innocent? What if there was still some different question none of them had thought to ask?

He turned to Rawlins. He was limited now. This was not his witness—he could only revisit the issues Busby had raised.

"How long have you been a surgeon with the regiment, sir?"

Busby was still standing. "Are you questioning Major Rawlins's qualifications?" he asked incredulously.

"Of course I'm not!" Narraway said extremely tartly. "I am trying to establish his very considerable expertise. Do you think I should be questioning his qualifications?" He invested the same haughty disbelief into his own voice.

"For God's sake, man!" Busby exploded.

Latimer banged on the table. "Captain Busby! We will not have the Lord's name taken in vain in this court. We may be far from home, but that is all the greater reason to conduct ourselves with dignity. You will please allow Lieutenant Narraway to ask his questions. If they are inappropriate, then I shall tell him so."

A flash of anger spread up Busby's face, but he sat down.

Narraway was about to thank Latimer, then thought better of it. It would be rubbing in the point, probably unwisely. He merely inclined his head and turned again toward Rawlins.

"How long have you been a surgeon with the regiment, sir?" he repeated.

"Seven and a half years," Rawlins replied.

"And have you always had medical orderlies, such as John Tallis?"

"Yes, of course."

"How long have you had John Tallis, specifically?"

"Approximately two years."

"How has his conduct been, during that time?" Narraway could feel his heart pounding in his chest and his breath catching. He did not know what Rawlins's answer would be.

Rawlins stood a little straighter, squaring his shoulders. A tiny muscle ticked in his temple. His fair skin was sunburned, in places badly. He looked desperately tired.

"I found him undisciplined," he said quietly. "His sense of humor was unreliable, to put it at its kindest. He was frequently insubordinate. He was also the best medical orderly I have ever had, and I tried to encourage him to qualify as a doctor. He is highly skilled. He never gave up on saving a man's life or attempting to save a limb. His compassion is extraordinary. He drove some of the more rigid officers to distraction, but I never met an ordinary man, Indian or white, who did not like him. I realize that is not necessarily what you want to hear, but it is the truth."

At the table, Latimer closed his eyes. His face was bleak, reflecting the hurt of betrayal that he felt.

Narraway did not know what to say. The air in the room seemed too heavy to breathe in. His own mouth was dry. He could not look at Tallis. Rawlins clearly not only thought unusually highly of Tallis, he liked the man. This made Tallis's perceived betrayal a profoundly personal one, perhaps even more than it was professional, to the army and the country they both served.

Everyone was looking at Narraway, waiting for him to continue.

He gulped. He must say something.

"Did Corporal Tallis know Dhuleep Singh, as far as you are aware? Did he ever mention him, or did you see them together, Major Rawlins?"

"No."

"Can you imagine any reason whatever why Tallis should want to rescue Dhuleep Singh?"

"No."

"Corporal Tallis is charged with this crime not because we believe he did such a thing, but simply because it does not appear possible that anyone else could've. It is an accident of exclusion and not something we understand or can trace back to any behavior of Corporal Tallis. Do you know of any other reason why we should think him guilty?"

"No."

"Had he any hatred toward any of the men on the patrol that was ambushed?"

Rawlins was startled. "Good God, no!"

"Did he even know who they were? Is he given that information?"

"No! We deal with them when they come back, not before they go," Rawlins said bitterly. "I don't know what the hell you're trying to suggest, but it is rubbish."

"That is exactly what I am trying to suggest," Narraway answered. "There is some major element to this that we have not yet grasped."

"If you are looking for sense in war, then you are even younger and more naïve than I thought," Rawlins said wearily. "If you outlive the disease, it will cure itself."

Narraway could think of nothing to say to that. He thanked Rawlins and sat down.

It was still early, but Busby asked permission to delay calling Major Strafford until the following day, as he had a great deal of evidence to give. There might be a way, with some consideration, of shortening it without impairing the course of justice. Latimer agreed, and they adjourned by half-past four.

Narraway walked out into the waning afternoon. He felt dazed, and he ached as if he had been in a physical fight. He had only this evening in which to come up with any witness to call for a defense when Strafford was finished testifying as to his investigation.

Tallis himself was no help. He still insisted that he had no idea who could have helped Dhuleep Singh escape, only that it hadn't been him.

Unless he could find that missing piece tonight, Narraway had nothing left except to challenge the witnesses Strafford's questioning produced. He could imagine how successful that was likely to be. No one was going to admit to mistakes or go back on what they had first said. Continual repeating of it would have made it indelible in their minds, even if it had originally been tentative. Uncertainty would be wiped out by saying over and over again "I saw" or "I was there." Even if doubt came, who would admit it now, with the Court looking on and the whole regiment watching?

He was walking across the open space beyond the rooms where the trial was held. The sky in the east was darkening, and little whispers of wind were stirring up eddies in the dust. Children were shouting in the distance, playing a game of some sort. A group of women stood close together, heads bent as they talked. Someone laughed: a soft, startlingly agreeable sound.

"Narraway!" a voice called out abruptly from behind him.

He turned and saw Strafford a dozen yards away, moving quickly, his boots sending up spurts of dust.

"Yes, sir?" Narraway answered obediently. This was a confrontation he would dearly like to avoid, but Strafford outranked him and so he had no escape.

Strafford reached him and stopped. He looked awkward, but the muscles were tight in his jaw, and clearly he was not going to be put off.

"I intend to call the witnesses tomorrow who can rule out every man in Cawnpore, apart from Tallis," he said without preamble. "Don't drag this out any longer than you have to. You can question each one as much as you like, and I appreciate that you have to make it look as if you are attempting to defend the man. But you're new here—relatively new to India, for that matter. These men have been through hell. Every one of them has lost people he served with, people who've stood side by side with him in the face of the enemy." He swallowed. "Maybe you don't know what that means yet . . ."

Narraway stiffened. "I'm not a lawyer, sir, I'm a soldier," he said sharply. "I've fought in the line just like anyone else. I've seen men die—and worse than that, I've seen them horribly wounded. I don't mean to be insubordinate, sir, but you have no grounds and no right to assume that all I do is defend soldiers in a back room in some military post. I'm doing this because I was ordered to, not because I chose it."

"I know that, Narraway, damn it!" Strafford said angrily. "Who the hell do you think chose you? Latimer doesn't know you from the clerk who writes up the dispatches home."

"Then he should bloody well look at the pips on my shoulders!" Narraway snapped.

Strafford almost smiled but stopped himself. "Would you prefer it if I said he doesn't know you from any other newly commissioned young officer fresh off the boat? I do, however, at least by repute."

Narraway's heart sank. Here was the issue of Strafford's brother again, the whole school record, the teasing, some of it less than good-natured, the inner contempt from the "swot" who preferred classics to sports—except cricket.

"Is that why you suggested to Colonel Latimer that he have me defend Tallis?" Narraway asked bitterly.

Strafford's eyebrows rose. "Did you think I picked your name out of a hat? Of course it is. You're a stubborn bastard, and you won't be beaten until you can see it so close in front of you you'll hit your nose if you take another step. Every man, no matter what he's accused of, deserves someone to speak for him. And right here and now, in this gutted town with its ground still reeking of blood, we need to be sure we're hanging the right man, and then we need to do it quickly. Fight, by all means, but when you're beaten, which will be tomorrow, give up. Don't give Tallis false hope. That's like a cat playing with a mouse. Let the end be quick and clean."

Narraway looked at Strafford, searching his face. He saw dislike in it, but not deceit.

"Are you absolutely certain Tallis is guilty?" he asked.

"Yes, I am," Strafford replied without hesitation. "I've looked into every other possibility, and it could have been no one else. Damn it, Narraway, the man may be an insubordinate clown, but he's one of the best medical orderlies I've ever seen. Men respect him. He's probably saved as many lives over the last couple of years as Rawlins himself. Do you think I'd pin this on him if there were any other man it could have been? I want the truth—and I wish this weren't it, but it is."

"Why?" Narraway asked stubbornly. "Why would Tallis rescue Dhuleep Singh? They didn't even know each other. If they did, you'd have produced a witness to say so."

"I don't know," Strafford admitted, miserable but not disconcerted. "Why do people do half the desperate or idiotic things they do? When you've been here another year or two, you won't ask questions like that. Where were you during the summer? Not here! Not watching men you know dying of heatstroke or cholera, getting weaker day by day, sharing what food and water there was, protecting the women, desperate to save them. You weren't here crouching behind that pathetic wall of earth, with nothing to shield you but a few bits of wood planking and some boxes, knowing that devil Nana Sahib was massing his hordes around you, growing closer every hour."

Narraway wanted to interrupt him, but he dared not.

"Some of these men have seen hell in a way few people ever do," Strafford went on. "Look in their faces sometime, Lieutenant. Look in their eyes, then come back and ask me why they do crazy things, or forget who they are or why they're here. Imagine what Tallis has seen, and ask me if he could have gone mad and acted in a way that makes no sense. Maybe he thought Chuttur Singh was Nana Sahib, or some other monster who cut up women and children. Maybe he simply lost his mind for a moment. I don't know. I just know that no one else could have done it. Believe me, I wish they could have. I tried to find any other answer."

Narraway felt as if he had suddenly tripped and fallen, or that the ground had risen up and struck him. Of course men who had endured what these men had could not be expected to keep the grip on sanity that men sitting comfortably at home could.

Tallis's clear blue eyes did not look insane. Desperate, perhaps, lit with an occasional, wild, mocking humor; but was that madness or the ultimate sanity? The only way to survive might be to take life a minute at a time, laugh when you could, weep when you had to.

"I saw the bodies of the men on the patrol," Strafford went on, his voice cracking from his effort to control it. "They were cut to bits too. I knew every one of them. I'm the one who had to tell their wives, lie a little and say it was quick, pretend they hadn't bled to death out there knowing no one would come for them or perhaps even find them before the animals had destroyed their bodies."

"I spoke to Tierney," Narraway said. "Actually, I spoke to him for quite a long time. Told him about Kent, where I come from, and he told me about his home. But sir, everything you said—all these terrible things that happened—I'm not going to add to that. I'm not going to give up until I don't have another step to go."

Strafford's face was grim. "My brother said you were a stubborn sod."

"Yes, sir," Narraway replied, standing to attention. "I don't suppose you want my opinion of him?"

"No, I bloody don't!" Strafford's face eased slightly. "I've got my own, better informed than yours."

Narraway relaxed a fraction, but not quite enough for Strafford to be certain of it, he hoped.

Strafford stared at him for a moment, then turned and walked away. He disappeared in another swirl of dust as the wind eddied more sharply, the bare branches of the trees above him clattering, a host of dry seedpods falling lightly to the ground.

Narraway also turned, but instead he walked farther away from the shattered barracks and the entrenchment, away from the Bibighar Gardens and the clustered outbuildings and the beginning of the houses. He must think of something to say tomorrow. Strafford Minor had called him stubborn but not fit to make a good soldier, all brains and no courage, no steel in the soul. He knew that because he had said it to Narraway's face, at Eton.

Well, he would prove that Strafford Minor was wrong.

IN THE MORNING, BUSBY CALLED MAJOR STRAFFORD TO give evidence. He began by establishing that it was Strafford who had been commanded to investigate the murder of Chuttur Singh, which was a direct result of Dhuleep Singh's escape.

Then he drew in a deep breath. "I regret the necessity for going into detail in this, but you were the officer entrusted with conducting the investigation into this act that has cost the lives of ten men and will yet take the life of whoever is guilty of perpetrating it. Colonel Latimer has known you and your record for years, but his companion judges may be less familiar with exactly what manner of man you are. I say this because they are going to accept your honor, integrity, and diligence as evidence of other men's actions and pass their verdict accordingly."

Strafford did not reply.

"It is a matter of record that you have served in the Indian Army for eleven years, with distinction. Were you here during the siege last summer?"

Strafford stiffened, and his face paled. "Yes."

"You must have seen an appalling amount of suffering and death."

"Yes."

"During that time, did you know the surgeon, Major Rawlins?"

"Of course."

"And Corporal Tallis, his medical orderly?"

Strafford was clearly distressed by the question. He licked his lips and coughed before replying.

"Of course I did. Before you ask me, he was an excellent orderly, often performing duties far beyond the requirements of his office or his training. Any man here will tell you that." He took a deep breath. "Believe me, I hate having to conclude that he is guilty of orchestrating Dhuleep Singh's escape. I did everything I could to find any other answer at all. I failed, because there is no other."

Busby stood ramrod stiff, carefully avoiding Narraway's eyes and Latimer's.

138

"Major Strafford, I need to ask you, so no one is in any doubt whatsoever regarding your personal feelings: Have you at any time had cause to dislike Corporal Tallis? We are all aware that on occasion he has been known to be . . . insubordinate, to have a sense of humor that is somewhat unfortunate, given to rather childish practical jokes on those he considers to be . . . stiffer in their command than he judges to be warranted. Has he ever played any of these rather childish jokes on you? Perhaps caused others to have less respect for you than is right? In other words, have you ever been the butt of his humor? Have you been laughed at, made fun of, had your authority belittled?"

"No."

"I see. Major Strafford, I know it is difficult, but can you describe your experience of what happened here at the end of the siege?"

A dull flush spread up Strafford's lean face. "For God's sake, man!" He all but choked on his words. "We were both there when Mrs. Greenway came with the note from Nana Sahib, offering on oath and treaty to give safe passage for the wounded, the women and the children, across the Ganges and then to Allahabad. In return he asked for and was given all the money, stores, and guns in the entrenchment." His voice shook, and he had difficulty continuing.

Narraway sat frozen, not in misery for Tallis but for Strafford himself.

Busby waited.

Strafford controlled himself with a fierce effort, drawing in breath again and again. His face was ashen.

"On the morning of the twenty-seventh, those of us left went from the entrenchment to the boats. There were Indian soldiers lining the banks."

Busby shifted his weight. No one else in the room made even the slightest sound.

"You know what happened after that," Strafford said, his voice so constricted in his throat that he could barely form the words. "Tantia Topee ordered the bugle sounded, then two guns were pulled out of concealment and opened fire on the boats, with grapeshot, followed by the muskets." The tears were running freely down his face now, and he made no effort to conceal them. "The thatch on the boats caught fire. The wounded and the helpless were burned to death. Some of the women, including my own wife, leaped into the river with their children. They too were shot, or cut down by the sabers of the troopers who rode their horses into the water and slaughtered all but a few. The men who made it to the shore were killed there, the women and children taken prisoners."

The room was silent.

Finally, Latimer spoke. "Nothing we can say will ease such horror. It is all a man needs to know of hell. I presume you have some purpose, Captain Busby, in obliging Major Strafford to relive his loss?"

Busby swallowed. "Yes, sir. Major Strafford, during all this horror, and afterward, what was Corporal Tallis's role, to your knowledge?"

Narraway was stunned. He had no idea what to do. The course of the trial had slipped uncontrollably out of his hands. He looked at Tallis and saw tears on his face also.

"He was with the wounded and among the last to embark," Strafford answered. "He did everything he could to help those further attacked. No man exhibited more selfless courage than he did."

"So it must hurt and dismay you, as much as it does Major Rawlins, to be forced to come to the conclusion that Corporal Tallis, and only Corporal Tallis, could have released Dhuleep Singh? And that it is possible that Corporal Tallis could've been the one to murder Chuttur Singh?"

"Yes."

Busby gave a slight shrug. "Just in case anybody should think of it, is there any chance that Chuttur Singh was part of that hideous massacre? Could Tallis have had revenge for it in his mind?"

"No," Strafford said flatly. "Chuttur Singh was loyal all his life. I know that for a fact. No one could have thought differently."

"Thank you. Now let us continue with your detailed evidence of the day of Dhuleep's escape and Chuttur's murder," Busby continued. "What evidence did you find that immediately implicated anyone?"

"None," Strafford replied. "Chuttur Singh had died without naming anyone, and the men who answered the alarm were too late to catch sight of anyone, even when they went after Dhuleep."

"So what did you do?" Busby asked. They all knew what Strafford was going to say.

Strafford sounded tired, and there were lines of fatigue in his face. "I started questioning the other men who had been on duty—or off duty, but in the general area—at the time. They could all account for their whereabouts, except Corporal Tallis." His jaw was tight, as if every muscle was clenched.

Busby looked apologetic. "Since Corporal Tallis has denied any involvement in either the escape or the murder, I'm afraid that obliges me to ask you for the details of your investigation. Lieutenant Narraway has informed me that he will not accept your assurance, as I had hoped he might, and save us this miserable exercise. God knows, we have enough else to do."

Narraway rose to his feet, driven by anger rather than sense. "Is Captain Busby suggesting that we hang a man for a crime of which he may be innocent, in order to save the time it takes to go through the procedure of a trial, sir?"

Latimer's lips thinned, and his hands on the tabletop were rigid. "Of course not!" he snapped, turning to Busby. "Captain, your choice of words was clumsy, to put it at its kindest. It is you who is wasting time with this grandstanding. Move on."

Busby flushed with anger. He dared not retaliate,

but neither would he apologize. He turned to Strafford again.

"Would you please give us an account of the various steps you took in your investigation, and how you ruled out all the possible suspects apart from Corporal Tallis?"

In a flat voice Strafford obeyed, listing all the men he had confirmed were in the immediate area of the prison. He had a sheet of paper with names, and he read them aloud.

"We know to the minute the time of the escape," he continued. "Most of these men were within sight of several people, and it was a simple matter to be certain beyond any possible doubt that they could not have been anywhere near the prison. In all cases the officer in charge at the time will swear to those accounted for, if you wish."

Before Busby could say anything, Latimer spoke.

"If that satisfied you, Major Strafford, it satisfies the Court. Who did it leave unaccounted for?"

Strafford looked at his list. "Corporal Reilly, Lance-Corporal McLeod, Privates Scott, Carpenter, and Avery, and Corporal Tallis, sir."

"Thank you. So that Lieutenant Narraway might question them also, if he feels there is some point to it, perhaps we had better hear from them directly." He glanced sideways at Narraway, as if to be certain the Court knew that it was Narraway who was dragging out the proceedings unnecessarily.

"Yes, sir, if you please," Narraway replied, as if it were Latimer who had asked.

Scott was the first called. In response to Busby's careful direction, he accounted for his duties and his movements on the day of Chuttur's death. He had been across the open yard and around a dogleg from the prison. But anyone coming or going would have had to pass him, because that was the only access to the front, and there was no door at the back of the makeshift prison.

"What were you doing, Private Scott?"

"Working on mending a storeroom, sir. Door and windows had been smashed by shellfire during the siege. I was making it weatherproof again."

"With your back to the courtyard, then?" Busby asked.

"No, sir. During that time I was making a new frame

for the door. Had the wood up on a bench of sorts, planing it to fit."

"So you could see anyone passing in either direction?"

"Yes, sir."

"Could anyone see you?"

"Yes, sir. Lance-Corporal McLeod and Private Avery."

"And no one passed you? You swear to it?"

"Yes, sir."

"And you were there for that entire hour, Private Scott?"

"Yes, sir. It took me longer'n that to finish."

"And could you see Corporal Reilly from where you were?"

"Yes, sir."

"Did he move at all?"

"Yes, sir. 'E came over ter me ter see 'ow I were doing, an' 'e told me I weren't doin' it right. 'E showed me 'ow to."

"And then what?" Busby pressed.

" 'E went off be'ind me, to see 'ow the rest were gettin' on. Then 'e came back."

"In the direction of the prison block?"

"No, sir, other way, back toward the river."

"Is there a way he could have gone around—in a circle perhaps—and got to the prison block?"

"No, sir, not without passing the squad 'oo were over at the end o' the entrenchment, sir."

"And Private Carpenter?"

"He was opposite me, working with Corporal Reilly."

"All the time?"

"Yes, sir."

"Thank you." Busby turned to Narraway with a slight, ironic gesture of invitation.

Narraway accepted, playing for time rather than because he had any questions in mind. He hoped that something might come to him. Testimony had shown Tallis to be exactly the sort of man Narraway had thought him: brave; irreverent, with a completely irresponsible sense of humor; intensely compassionate; dedicated to medicine. But it also had been damning, because it was clear that if Strafford could have found any other answer, he would have.

Narraway stood facing Private Scott. Detail by detail, the soldier accounted for every move he had made, repeating what he had said before, not in parrot fashion, but as if clearly seeing it again in his mind's eye. Narraway achieved nothing at all.

It was exactly the same with Corporal Reilly, and then with Private Carpenter. Busby asked each of them where they had been. They each gave a sober account, in very slightly different words but amounting to the same evidence. In each case they supported one another, proving that none of them could have left their position, and the other's sight, long enough to have reached the prison block and gone inside it. Narraway began to feel as if he was wasting everyone's time, and he could see the truth of it in the growing impatience on the faces around him.

Tallis was looking more and more desperate, struggling to keep his composure and an appearance of some kind of hope. Narraway could only guess at the courage required for Tallis to sit there silently. Was he wasting everyone's time, drawing out the tension and pain pointlessly?

He thought of what Strafford had said of that terrible crossing with the boats on fire, the drowning and the dead, and Tallis wading in and risking his own life without a backward glance. Narraway could not give up yet, not until he was so beaten he had nowhere else to go.

Lance-Corporal McLeod came to the stand, and Busby questioned him also.

He was perhaps twenty-two, fair-skinned, pale. His eyes were hollow, staring far beyond Busby as if he saw something else, something printed indelibly on his memory.

"And where were you exactly, Corporal McLeod?" Busby prompted.

"On the corner, sir, just beyond the building that was pretty well smashed."

"In the southwest, correct?"

"Yes, sir."

"And you could see the door to the prison from where you were?"

"Yes, sir."

"Were you looking at it all the time?"

"No, sir. I was paying attention to what I was doing."

"Which was what, Corporal?"

"Mending a cart, sir. Shaft was broken."

"Was anyone helping you?"

"Yes, sir, Private Avery. Too heavy for one man, at least when it comes to lifting it together to weld."

"And could you see Corporal Reilly and Private Scott working on the storeroom?"

"Yes, sir."

"All the time? Are you certain?"

"Corporal Reilly could have gone the other way, sir, but not past me toward the prison, sir. Private Avery or I would have seen him."

"Thank you. Please stay there so Lieutenant Narraway can ask you . . . whatever it is he needs to." Busby did not hide the fact that he regarded this as a cruel and pointless waste of not only time but emotion. All around them was the air of danger, of hate, the bitter knowledge that fighting was going on just beyond their hearing and sight. All of northern India was in turmoil. Friends and allies were dying to save what was left of British rule, and here they were, locked up in this tiny room, arguing over a truth everyone knew perfectly well. All it really needed was to be faced, the bitter acceptance made and dealt with. Courage was necessary, not more talk, more weighing and measuring of what they all knew. In a sense it was like vultures fighting over a corpse. Busby had not said so, not in so many words, but he had more than implied it.

Narraway did not ask McLeod anything. He knew he had tried Latimer's patience as far as it would go.

The last witness was Private Avery.

Busby stood and faced him patiently.

"Private, would you describe to us exactly where you were at the time Chuttur Singh was killed? We have been over this before. All you need to do is recall what you told me then and tell me again, so the Court can hear you."

Obediently, as if he were reciting some ritual litany, Avery told him exactly where he had been and what had occupied him. He seemed stunned. Narraway thought that the man blamed himself for not having seen something that could have saved Chuttur Singh, as if it had been his fault that he had been so near and done nothing to prevent the killing.

When it was Narraway's turn to question him, he felt like he could not ask the man to repeat it all again—it would be brutal.

"Think carefully, Private Avery: Have you left anything out? If not, there is no need for me to go over it again."

"Nothing, sir," Avery answered. "That's how it was. I'm sorry, sir."

"Just one thing that Captain Busby didn't ask you: Do you know Corporal Tallis?"

Avery's face went even paler. "Yes, sir."

"How do you know him?"

"I got a bullet wound in the arm, sir. Not very bad, but it bled a lot. Corporal Tallis stitched it up for me."

"Corporal Tallis did, not Major Rawlins?" Narraway said with surprise.

"Dr. Rawlins was busy with someone a lot worse hurt than me, sir."

"I see. Did Corporal Tallis make a good job of it?"

"Yes, sir, very good. Healed up real well. And . . ." He stopped, looked at the floor. "There was a lot of blood, sir. I was scared. He made me laugh, and I felt as if it would be all right. It—it was the first time I'd been hit . . . sir."

"So you know Corporal Tallis?"

"Yes, sir." Avery looked so wretched, it was as if he were in physical pain.

"Could you see the door of the prison from where you were working?"

"Yes, sir."

"Did you see him during that hour? Did you see him anywhere near the prison?"

"No, sir."

"Thank you." Narraway sat down again because he could think of nothing further to say.

Latimer adjourned the Court, and Narraway walked out into the late afternoon. The sun was sinking low to the horizon, painting the west with burning color. The coming night had already shrouded the east, spreading a veil of shadow across the sky. He felt as if the darkness were enclosing him, wrapping around him and reaching inside.

It was a time not to be alone.

And yet only in solitude could he even attempt to concentrate his mind. Nothing so far helped. Every piece of testimony proved that no one else could have gone in through the prison door. And more than that, no one had an ill word to say about Tallis. None of them wished to believe him guilty.

Strafford's evidence had been even worse than Rawlins's. He was a good man desperately bereaved, who had nevertheless done his duty without expecting anyone else to ease his burden. He had not wanted Tallis to be guilty. It betrayed everything he had trusted, even the past help that Tallis had been to him personally.

Did all this make Strafford doubt his own judgment now? If he could trust and admire a man and be so bitterly mistaken, could he have faith in himself in any other judgment? If Tallis could be so infinitely less than his estimation, then who else might also be?

And if Strafford, with his knowledge, could be wrong, why on earth did Narraway imagine that he was any better? He barely knew Tallis. He liked his humor and admired his courage. But Strafford had known the man, day in and day out, for years. He had seen his work. They had faced horror and the final, rending grief of loss together. But he'd also had the courage to accept that Tallis was guilty. What must that have cost him?

Narraway could not shake the evidence. No one was lying; no combination of men had conspired to make the situation look this way.

Perhaps Strafford was not being sarcastic when he said he had chosen Narraway because he believed in his stubbornness and intelligence. Maybe he really did—and far from ending up feeling furious and duped, if Narraway could find a way out, a way to restore their faith in Tallis and thus in their own judgment, Strafford would be intensely grateful?

If that was the case, then by failing he was not only letting Tallis die, he was also letting down the whole regiment. It was a lonely and terrible thing to live without the faith you had once leaned on when all else was broken. Death might not be preferable, but there must be times, like at two o'clock in the morning, when it seemed a whole lot easier.

And there were women and children left without their men—like the widow whose shopping he had carried and whose little girl had given him her blue paper chain, made for a Christmas her brother had said was for everybody.

Then, suddenly, he was ashamed of his own self-absorption. Whoever was betrayed, bereaved, accused falsely or not, it was not he. He was supposed to be part of the resolution, the one who fought for justice, whether that was Tallis's vindication or his death.

He was still walking, aimlessly. He had intended to

go to his own house and spend the evening revising all that he had learned so far, in the hope that some inconsistency would emerge or some new fact or deduction would appear.

However, as he walked along the road, he found himself turning aside from the way to his own bungalow and going instead toward the house of the widow with the little girl who had given him the blue paper chain.

It was almost dusk, and night would come quickly, as it always did in India. There was no lingering twilight of the north here. Soon there would be lights in the windows. Women would begin to cook an evening meal. The comfortable smells of food would fill the air. It would only be after the children had gone to bed that they would sit in the empty rooms downstairs and face the long aloneness of the night.

Helena was sitting on the front steps, holding a doll in her arms and talking to it. She became aware of him standing at the gate and looked up. She smiled at him shyly.

He remained where he was, smiling back at her.

The woman came to the door. He had learned that her name was Olivia Barber. Perhaps she had seen him from the window and had come to make sure her child was safe.

"Good evening, Lieutenant," she said, clearly enough for him to hear her from where he was.

"Good evening, ma'am," he replied. "I beg your pardon for disturbing you."

"It's supper time," Helena said, still staring at him. "Are you here for supper?"

He felt embarrassed, as if he had tried to invite himself in.

Olivia put her hand on the child's shoulder, pulling her back a little. "You are welcome to join us, if you would like, Lieutenant," she said quietly. "I apologize for Helena's forwardness."

He felt even more awkward, but he very much wanted to accept. He wanted the comfort, the normality of it. And he would love, above all else, to forget defeat for an hour or two.

"Are you sure it will not inconvenience you?" he asked hesitantly.

"I'm quite sure," she answered, opening the door a little wider behind her.

He went up the path and inside, Helena watching him carefully all the way. He wondered with a flash of pain if she understood yet that her father was never coming home. Was she too young for that? Had her mother even tried to explain it?

Inside, the house was warm and tidy, full of the smells of cooking, clean laundry and some kind of polish. There were a few toys on the floor, not many. He was pleased to see that there was no wagon. But then, perhaps at five David was too big for such things? Should he ask, or was that clumsy?

The food was not ready yet. He was invited to sit down.

"Aren't you going to play with me?" Helena looked disappointed. "David's reading."

"Helena!" Olivia said chidingly. "The lieutenant has been working all day. He's tired."

Helena's face crumpled.

"I'd love to play with you," Narraway said quickly. "What game would you like?"

He was rewarded with a beaming smile. "Hide-and-seek," she said immediately.

"Helena . . ." her mother began, but the little girl was already running away, giggling with excitement.

Narraway stood up. "Where should I look for her?" he asked quietly. "I don't want to find her too soon. Please tell me where it's all right for me to try."

Olivia laughed and gave a slight shrug. "Anywhere in this half of the house," she replied. "You're fairly safe to try behind all the doors and in the cupboards. She hardly ever hides there."

"Thank you." He set off uncertainly. This was a house in which he was a guest, a woman's house, full of personal and family things. It would be inexcusable to intrude. To start with, he moved tentatively, silently, then he realized it would be no fun for Helena if she could not hear him looking, puzzled, not finding her.

"I'm coming to find you!" he said clearly. He went out into the central entranceway. "I think you're in the coat cupboard." He opened the door and was relieved to see nothing but coats and capes. He closed it again and saw a boot box. "Could you be in there?" he said. "Far too small—but maybe!" He opened it, sighed, and closed it again. "No. Then where can you be?"

He kept it up, with a running commentary, going to one room after another and still not finding her. Finally there was only one room left, which was clearly her bedroom. He opened it tentatively, afraid of intruding.

"She can't be in here," he said aloud. "It isn't bedtime yet." He looked around. The small bed was neatly made, except for a coverlet dropped on the floor. She wasn't here. He was perplexed. He thought he had looked everywhere that had been suggested, excluding only the other bedrooms—Olivia's and the one where David was reading.

"I give up!" he said dramatically. "She's gone!"

There was a giggle from the coverlet on the floor, and very slowly a tousled little girl squirmed out of it, leaving it in exactly the same shape. Her face was alight with victory, eyes shining.

"I won!" she said happily. "You didn't find me! I'm hungry. Let's go down for supper." Dancing from one foot to the other, she led the way.

Narraway followed her to the dining room and took his place at the table, opposite David, already there. He felt awkward then. He appreciated the welcome but was acutely aware that he was in another man's place. So much of the warmth was a pretense, meant to comfort them all for a short time. It was a game that gave a few hours' respite from reality.

They spoke of other times and places, not India. Christmases past, the day with its promise of hope for those with the courage to accept its message and believe it.

But when the housemaid came to take David and Helena to bed and they had all said good night, Narraway remained a little longer in the quiet room. Now that pretense had ended, he could see how tired Olivia was, what an effort it cost her to always hide her grief from them so they would not know how much everything had changed. War raged around them in every direction, but they were not afraid because, to them, she was not afraid.

Suddenly his troubles seemed very small.

"Thank you," he said sincerely. "You have reminded me of the sanity of things that last, and that they are not always bought cheaply."

She looked at him in surprise, not quite sure what he meant. The meal had been simple, mostly rice.

He seized on the first thing that came to his mind. "Have you any more garlands, paper chains? Perhaps I can help you put them up?"

"Lieutenant, they're only—"

"It'll need two of us," he pointed out. "One at each end. Wouldn't the children like to see them all up when they come down in the morning?"

"You don't have to . . ." she began.

"I'd like to. We shouldn't ever forget Christmas, or make little of it. We give presents when we can, but there's no gift as precious as Christmas itself." He stopped, feeling self-conscious.

She smiled at him and stood up. "You're quite right. Of course I'd love you to help hang the garlands up. We have five or six, and there are some wreaths of dried flowers, and ribbons."

She fetched them, and together they put them up with pins and tacks—not always very straight, but an hour later, when they were finished, the room was transformed. As far as Narraway was concerned, it was like nailing your flags to the mast, a statement of hope.

"Do you think they'll like it?" he asked, looking carefully at her face, seeing the light in it again, even a hint of laughter.

"They'll love it," she said without hesitation. "I think I shall pretend to be as surprised as they'll be, if you don't mind?"

"An excellent idea," he agreed.

"Would you like a cup of tea before you go?" she said with a smile.

"Thank you, I really would," he answered, following her into the kitchen while she made it.

Afterward, thanking her again, Narraway went out into the darkness, smiling.

Far above him, a flight of birds crossed the clear night sky and circled down toward the trees. There always seemed to be birds, except over the ruined part of the town—lots of different kinds, unfamiliar to him. He loved their easy flight, which gave an illusion of freedom, an almost magical ability to rise above anything and be wherever or whatever you wished.

He knew perfectly well they were as subject to hunger, cold, exhaustion, and predators as anyone else, but the momentary illusion was still worth something.

He would have to call all the witnesses again and find some discrepancy, some error or contradiction. He hated the thought of arguing and trying to trip them up. The only thing that would be worse was letting Tallis be hanged without giving it the best fight he could.

And that brought him to the fact that he could no longer put off going to see Tallis, perhaps for the last time. The wind was rising a little whispering, murmuring. It was nearly dark, no more birds left in the sky, just a thin ribbon of red fading in the west.

And then suddenly he had an idea—tremulous as the last light, elusive, but perhaps possible!

FOR A FEW MOMENTS, HE THOUGHT THE TIRED GUARD would refuse to allow him in. However, he looked again at Narraway's face, at his eyes, and must have decided that arguing with him would be a great deal more trouble than simply giving in.

Tallis was lying on his back on the bunk, eyes wide open. He stood up as Narraway came in. He was even paler than before, and there were bruises on his skin.

"You look terrible," Narraway said with some concern. "Can I get Rawlins for you?"

Tallis's face broke into a smile. "I like your sense of humor, Lieutenant. I couldn't have done better than that myself. To do what? You have to wait until the patient is dead before you certify it. Or have you given up on proving me innocent, and you're going to smuggle me out as already dead and say I escaped? Stupid, but I like a man who doesn't know when he's beaten."

Narraway heard the edge in his voice, the fear just under the surface. "I was actually going to suggest that he give you something to make you look better, even if you don't feel it," he replied, making an effort to smile back. "I intend to finish the course, whether there's any point to it or not. It's one thing to be beaten; it's another to give up."

"It won't do your career any good," Tallis observed.

"Sit down before you fall over," Narraway told him. "I may need your answers tomorrow."

"It won't make any difference," Tallis assured him. "In civilian life they think twice about hanging a sick man, but in the army they don't give a damn. You can be missing arms and your legs be out cold, and some helpful bastard'll tie you up so they can still put the noose around your neck."

"Thank you," Narraway said wryly. "If I'm ever accused back at home, I'll remember to be ill at the time. Now sit down and try to pay attention."

Tallis sat. In fact, it was more of an overbalancing because he had temporarily forgotten there was no chair, only the mattress on the ground. He looked up at Narraway, a flare of hope in his eyes for a moment before he remembered to disguise it.

"Did you kill Chuttur Singh?" Narraway asked.

"No."

"Did you release Dhuleep?"

"No."

"What do you know about him? And don't tell me 'nothing.' You've treated half the men in this regiment. I need you to tell me everything you know about him, whether you think it's relevant or not. I don't care if it's military-related, personal, or medical. It's not just your life that depends on it; it's the matter of finding the man who did this, if it isn't you. It's about saving some kind of honor for the regiment. Unless you're covering for someone for that very reason."

Tallis looked amazed. Then laughter welled up in him, and died instantly.

"No," he said croakily. "I'm not noble enough to swing on a rope for a crime I didn't commit, if that's what you think. I don't want to be executed out here and my name to go down as traitor." He blinked rapidly, trying to stop his eyes from filling with tears. "I don't want my family to live with that . . . my mother. She was once . . . terribly proud of me . . ."

Narraway found his own throat tight. He refused to allow in thoughts of his last parting with his own mother. She was a woman of immense elegance and quiet, very private but passionate, just as he was.

"Then tell me!" he said in sudden fury, sitting down on the floor, opposite Tallis. "Tell me everything you know about Chuttur Singh and Dhuleep Singh. And be quick. I've only got tonight, and I'd like to get enough sleep to be able to stand straight in court and not need anyone to prop me up. It won't make any difference if you collapse, but it might if I do!"

"No, it won't," Tallis said quickly. "Not really. It'll just look silly."

"Now, Corporal!" Narraway snapped. "Tell me every

last detail you know about Dhuleep and Chuttur. You've got until midnight."

"What are you going to do at midnight?" Tallis asked curiously. "You need a hell of a lot of sleep, for a young and supposedly healthy soldier."

"I'm going to find out more about these men and put the pieces together, of course! Paint a different picture. So, Corporal Tallis, get on with it."

But Tallis could tell Narraway little more than he already knew. He only drew more vividly the horror and the exhaustion of the last few months. There was no anger in him, except at the circumstances that cost young men their lives, and seemingly for so little in return. There was pity and wry, twisting humor here, between the men, snatches of companionship, gulfs of loneliness and, always at the back of it, a courage that climbed up to its feet every time it was beaten down.

Nothing Tallis said made the new theory in Narraway's mind impossible, and at midnight, as he had promised, he left Tallis and began finding the other men, waking them up if necessary, asking the same questions of all of them.

What had Dhuleep been like as a soldier, as a man?

Obviously he was a Sikh. Some Sikhs had remained loyal to the British, some had joined the mutiny. Why had he changed sides, and—more urgently—why had no one noticed? Was he guilty of the charge for which he was imprisoned?

"Yes—and for theft earlier on," one weary sergeant told him, sitting half asleep in the canteen. He was blinking at Narraway with a better temper than Narraway would have shown if he had been woken up at two in the morning by some man senior to him in rank but years junior in experience.

"Theft of what?" Narraway asked.

"Medicines, I think," the sergeant replied. "Quinine, stuff like that."

"To sell? To use on others? Did he need it himself?" Narraway was interested because it was an indication of Dhuleep's character and opportunism.

"Not that much!" the sergeant said with a twisted smile. "God knows what he wanted it for. He wouldn't say. Could have been to sell, or to take to the mutineers, to give to his friends or allies, or simply to rob us of the use of it."

"Could Tallis have been in on it?" It was a question

he really did not want the answer to, but he dared not evade it. "For profit?" he added.

"No," the sergeant said without hesitation. "It was Tallis who reported the theft. If he'd waited, we probably wouldn't have known who did it—or got it back, for that matter."

"So you caught Dhuleep Singh because of Tallis?"

"I suppose so. But it wasn't Tallis as got 'im, it was a couple of regulars called . . . Johnson was one of 'em. I think the other was Robinson, or Roberts. Something like that."

"What sort of a man was Dhuleep, before the theft?"

"Dunno. Ordinary, I think. Bit of a sneaky sod, but a good enough soldier. At least he seemed that way. If 'e ever stole before, 'e got away with it."

"Why was there only one guard looking after Dhuleep?" Narraway asked.

" 'Cos 'e were just a miserable layabout, an' 'e were locked up tight in a cell anyway. Probably wouldn't 'ave bothered locking 'im up, if it 'adn't been the medicines 'e took."

"Thank you." Narraway stood up. "I'd better go look

over all this past evidence and see if I can make any-thing different of it."

The sergeant stood as well, a big man, broad-chested, his shoulders sagging with weariness. "Ye're a tryer, I'll say that for yer. Don't give up, do yer?"

"Not till it's over," Narraway answered, finding the praise both bitter and welcome.

A N HOUR LATER, NARRAWAY HAD GONE OVER ALL THE evidence yet again when he suddenly came across what looked like an inconsistency between what Corporal Reilly had said and Private Carpenter's account. It was very tiny: just something in the order of events. He looked at his notes, reread them to make sure it was not his own hasty writing misleading him.

Corporal Reilly had said that he had been standing at the corner, where he could see Scott on the far side of the courtyard, planing the wood for the new door, and McLeod and Avery in the corner opposite, with a clear view of the prison entrance a hundred yards away to their left.

He also said that Carpenter had been there the entire time with him, as was borne out by all three of the others.

But if Reilly was right, and his account matched Scott's, then Carpenter was lying. He had backed up McLeod and Avery, when actually they must have been out of his sight, in the direction of the prison. It was a very small discrepancy, but they could not all be correct. Was it just an error by a man too tired, too shaken to remember accurately? Did it even matter now? Not if his own idea was right. But what if it wasn't? He could not afford to rely on it. If it was wrong, he must have something to fall back on. They had all sworn that their time was accounted for and that no one else could have gone into the prison before Grant led the response to the alarm.

He must waken Carpenter right now and get some explanation. Tallis's life could depend on it.

Narraway crossed the open space to the remnants of the barracks where Carpenter was billeted and found him with some difficulty. He had to explain to a guard who he was and that his errand could not wait. He expected to find Carpenter asleep. Instead, the man was lying uncomfortably on a straw mattress, tossing fitfully. He sat up as soon as he was aware of Narraway's presence in the room.

Narraway apologized immediately. He kept his voice as quiet as he could make it, so as not to disturb the other men who were within earshot and might also sleep lightly.

"I need to speak to you before the trial resumes tomorrow. Privately."

"What?" Carpenter was dazed. "Lieutenant? You're going to call me again?" He pushed his hand through his hair and sat up a little further. "What for?"

"Can we go outside?" Narraway asked. He phrased it as a request, but it was in effect an order.

In silence Carpenter stood up, pulled on his trousers and tunic, and followed Narraway outside into the night. The clear sky's blaze of stars gave little light, and the wind was higher than before, scraping the branches and rattling the leaves on the tamarind trees twenty feet away.

"What is it, sir?" Carpenter asked, shivering a little.

Narraway went over Carpenter's evidence step by step. He knew it by heart now. He repeated every moment, every word that accounted for someone else. Did it matter? He had no idea. He could not afford to let anything slip.

"Yes," Carpenter said wearily.

Narraway shook his head. "No," he denied quietly. "Not if Corporal Reilly was where he said he was, doing what he said he was doing. In that case, he would have been around the corner, out of sight of the prison. It can't be right. One of you has it wrong. Is that a mistake, or a lie? Think carefully before you decide, Private."

Carpenter stood motionless. Narraway's eyes were used to the dark, but even so he could see no expression on Carpenter's face.

Carpenter blinked several times, as if the dust eddies troubled him. He rubbed his arm over his face. Narraway waited. He felt guilty. There was no arrogance, no anger in the man in front of him, just an inner conflict he could not resolve.

"If you don't tell me the truth, Tallis may be hanged for something he didn't do," he said at last. "A good man, a man we need, will suffer an injustice we can't ever put right. Was it a mistake, Private Carpenter, or a lie?"

Carpenter chewed his lip.

Again Narraway waited. He thought for a moment that Carpenter had fallen asleep on his feet.

"It was a lie, sir." Carpenter's voice in the dark was painful, as if his mouth was too dry to form the words properly.

"Did you leave, or did Reilly?" Narraway asked, chilled now by the fact that what had been only a possibility—a straw to grasp for—had become a reality.

"I did, sir," Carpenter replied. He straightened up until his body was stiff. "I didn't see anything relevant to Dhuleep Singh's escape, sir. Nor did I see Corporal Tallis. I can't help with what happened, sir."

Narraway found that he was shivering too.

"I still want to know where you were," he said aloud.

Carpenter looked resigned, beaten. "I was with Ingalls, sir. Ingalls was . . . ill."

"Then Major Rawlins would know that," Narraway reasoned, wondering why Rawlins had said nothing earlier. Was it possible he did not know of Carpenter's testimony? That seemed hard to believe.

"Private Carpenter!" he said sharply.

"Yes, sir?" Carpenter stiffened.

" 'Yes, sir, Rawlins knows of this,' or just, 'Yes, sir, I am paying attention'?" Narraway demanded.

"Yes, sir . . . I am paying attention. No, sir, Major Rawlins doesn't know. It was . . . it wasn't that kind of illness . . ."

"You mean he was drunk? Why didn't he just sleep it off, like anyone else?" Narraway was puzzled, even disturbed. "Carpenter! You'd better tell me the truth now, rather than have me drag it out of you, and this Ingalls, in court in a few hours' time."

"Yes, sir." Carpenter's body sagged, as if he no longer had the strength or the will to stand upright.

Narraway took him by the arm. The private's flesh was cold even through his tunic. "Here. For God's sake come and sit down, and tell me what was wrong with Ingalls and why you went to him rather than call a doctor."

Carpenter stopped resisting. Together they walked over to a heap of rubble still lying piled up from the bombardment of the siege. For a moment or two Carpenter sat bent forward, composing his thoughts, then he began to speak.

"Ingalls drinks . . . badly. He was right out of it that

day. Jones covered for him. We always do." He did not look at Narraway. "But he couldn't handle this. Ingalls was worse than usual. He was shaking like a leaf and sobbing. Jones couldn't keep him from yelling out. In his own mind, Ingalls must've been miles away, in another world, back in the time when we first came in after the siege. He was one of the ones who found the bodies in the well at Bibighar. They swore an oath then, and he thinks he's betrayed it because he . . ." He stopped, lowering his head into his hands.

"What?" Narraway asked, feeling brutal. He was afraid of what he was going to hear. "I have to know if I'm going to help Tallis," he insisted.

"He would get delirious," Carpenter said. "See it all again, smell the blood, hear the flies. Tallis used to help him sometimes, you know. Made him laugh." He twisted around to face Narraway for a moment. "You've got to help Tallis, sir. I don't know what the hell happened, but he couldn't have done it, unless he had a reason—I mean, one he couldn't get out of, one that . . ." He turned away again and fell silent.

"So you went to Ingalls that day? Because Jones couldn't handle it?" Narraway prodded him.

"Ingalls was out of it," Carpenter said. "He was going to kill himself. Said he'd failed. General Wheeler's daughter was haunting him. He could see her ghost everywhere."

"What?" Narraway gasped. "General Wheeler's daughter? What are you talking about, man?"

Carpenter looked at him.

"Why were you the one to go?" Narraway demanded.

"Because I was there too."

"Where?"

"In the Bibighar. She was one of the women they killed. We found her head. Somebody—I think it was Frazer—cut off her scalp and divided it up, a piece of it to every man. He told us to count the hairs on our piece and swear an oath to kill one mutineer for every hair. Ingalls couldn't do it. He tried . . ."

Narraway sat frozen, unaware of everything around him, the night wind in the tamarind branches, the dust devils stirring across the open ground, the starlight.

Carpenter moved a little, just shifting position. "What have we become, sir? Ingalls doesn't understand anymore. He asks over and over again what the hell we're doing here anyway. Never mind making the Indians into Christians, what are we making ourselves into? And you know what, sir? I can't answer him. I don't know what to do! Tell you the truth, that day I wished Tallis was there. He knew what to say, 'cos he'd make fun of it all and just be . . . gentle."

Narraway sat without moving or speaking. He wanted to save Tallis so badly it was like a physical pain inside him, as if something necessary for survival were missing and the emptiness was going to eat him away.

"Tallis, he wouldn't even say you were going to live if he knew you were going to die," Carpenter went on, his voice seeming almost disembodied in the darkness. "But if you were scared out of your wits, or so drunk you couldn't stand up, and seeing all kinds of things that weren't there, if you'd run away like an idiot and sat angry in a corner, hugging your knees and crying like you couldn't stop, he'd still talk to you like you were a man, and worth something."

"How long did you stay with Ingalls?" Narraway asked.

"Don't know. Until he calmed down and I was sure he'd sleep it off, and not cut his throat. Couldn't very well hide all the knives, could I?" He gave a sharp burst of laughter. "Tallis said that once: 'Let's hide all the knives and guns so no one'll kill themselves. 'Course, then they won't be able to kill one another either, but there are no perfect answers, eh?' And then he gave that crazy laugh of his." He let out a long sigh. "But that doesn't help, does it? I'd have sworn on my life he'd never hurt anyone. Reilly was there, and Scott only lied to save me. And I lied to save Ingalls the humiliation. Makes no difference to the fact that no one but Tallis could have got in there, because he was still the only one who had the chance."

He turned to Narraway, sitting up straighter. "Pity you can't hang Ingalls instead. He'd like it. It'd put him out of his misery. Tallis would've said that, and laughed. Except it's not funny, 'cos it's true. I can't help you, sir."

"I'm sorry for waking you," Narraway said quietly. "I thought for a few moments that I'd find something. Go back to bed. You might sleep. You have to sometime."

For several more moments Carpenter didn't move, then at last he rose to his feet, stiffly.

"Sorry, sir," he said, and before Narraway could reply, he stumbled away into the shadows and was lost.

Narraway sat uncomfortably on the rubble a few moments longer, then he stood up and walked slowly to his own quarters, and a few hours of oblivion before the battle.

❧

THE NEXT MORNING WAS STILL AND COLD. IT HAD NEVER been known to snow in Cawnpore, but it was easy to believe that the shortest day of the year was coming, and Christmas would be only a few days after that.

The small courtroom was grim. No one looked as if they had slept, and the very idea of celebrating anything like Christmas seemed absurd, an idea belonging to a different world.

Busby stood up.

"I have no more witnesses to call, sir." He addressed Latimer but included the other two officers in his gaze. "There is no question that Dhuleep Singh was released from his cell and Chuttur Singh was hacked to death. While it is possible Dhuleep killed Chuttur, I have demonstrated beyond any doubt that there was no one else who could have let Dhuleep out in the first place except Corporal John Tallis. I cannot offer any explanation for why he did so. Whether he was threatened, or bribed, or simply lost his sanity under the pressure of events, I don't know, nor do I believe that it matters. The facts remain."

Latimer nodded slowly, his face furrowed deep with unhappiness. He turned to Narraway. "Do you have anything you would like to say, or to ask, Lieutenant Narraway? It is your duty to offer anything you can on behalf of the prisoner."

Narraway stood up slowly. His brief sleep had been full of nightmares. His mouth was dry.

"Yes, sir." He swallowed. "Captain Busby has presented a powerful case for Corporal Tallis's guilt, but it rests solely on the fact that he was unable to find anyone else to blame. He has not shown that Corporal Tallis was actually seen at the time and the place, that he has behaved like a guilty man, or that he had any mark on him that would prove a fight: bruises, cuts, blood—not even a torn or stained uniform. He has given us no reason at all why Tallis should do such a thing, except in a bout of complete insanity, which must have come on without warning and went again without leaving any mark behind it. As Captain Busby admits, he simply has no one else to blame."

Busby stood up.

"Sit down, Captain," Latimer said grimly. "Your disagreement is taken for granted. Give the man his chance."

Busby's face tightened, but he did not speak again.

"Sir," Narraway resumed, "I believe there may be some explanation for all the facts we have other than Corporal Tallis's guilt, but I need to question the witnesses again, very precisely, before I can be certain. I have already found some errors and dismissed them after investigating more closely, because I found them to be unrelated to Dhuleep Singh's escape. I need now to explore certain other aspects that these errors may have thrown light upon." That was something of an exaggeration. He had no intention of telling them about Carpenter and Ingalls, but he had to make it sound as if he had a better cause for recalling witnesses than speculation, however plausible.

Latimer hesitated, seemed about to say something, then changed his mind. "Proceed, Lieutenant Narraway, but if you stray far from the point I shall stop you myself, never mind any objection Captain Busby may have."

"Yes, sir. I call Corporal Grant again."

Grant was duly reminded of his oath and, looking puzzled, faced Narraway.

The lieutenant was painfully aware that everyone in the room was looking at him with displeasure and a degree of suspicion. He avoided meeting Tallis's eyes.

"Corporal Grant . . ." Narraway stopped and cleared his throat. Suddenly his whole idea seemed absurd. He was going to make a complete fool of himself, ruin his career, disappoint Latimer, see Tallis hanged. He cleared his throat again. "Would you remind us where you were when you heard the prison alarm, and what you did? Please be absolutely exact, and if there is something you don't recall, say so. There is no shame in having your mind so bent in your duty, especially in times of emergency, that you don't notice other things."

Grant did as he was asked, slowly and carefully.

When he had finished, Narraway picked up the thread again, his voice shaking a little.

"The dying Chuttur Singh told you that the prisoner

had escaped," he confirmed. "That he had valuable information regarding the patrol, and that at all costs you should go after him. He himself was beyond help, even had you found a doctor for him, is that correct?"

"Yes, sir," Grant agreed. "I wanted to get help for Chuttur, but he insisted it was pointless and I should go after the prisoner." He looked distressed, his face flushed.

"And then Sergeant Attwood and Private Peterson arrived?" Narraway needed every last detail clear, exact.

"Yes, sir."

"Was it dark in the room? Was Chuttur's face splashed with blood?" He held his breath for the answer.

"Yes, sir," Grant answered, his voice wretched.

Busby rose to his feet, his face grim, his voice grating with anger. "Sir, these men all did exactly what they were trained to do, and what was the right thing. If the lieutenant is trying to suggest now that they were somehow mistaken and should have stayed with the man, when he was beyond all help, he is being cruel and is quite wrong. This only displays Lieutenant Narraway's inexperience, and—"

Latimer held up his hand. "Enough, Captain Busby. Your point is perfectly clear." He turned to Narraway. "Lieutenant, are you trying to suggest that any or all of these men should have tried to assist Chuttur Singh rather than go after the escaped prisoner? It was a judgment made in the heat of the moment, but I believe it was the correct one. Either way, what difference does it make to the guilt or innocence of John Tallis?"

Narraway felt the blood burn up his face. He knew he had sounded brutal, as if he were blaming Grant, but there was no other way. Please God, he was right!

"No, sir," he said, keeping his voice as steady as he could. "Grant, Attwood, and Peterson all behaved exactly as good soldiers should, sir. I intend no criticism at all. I just want to be absolutely certain, beyond any doubt at all, that that's what they did."

"If you do not reach some point soon, I shall be obliged to stop you for wasting our time," Latimer warned. "Get on with it."

Narraway turned to Grant again. "All of you left in pursuit of the escaped prisoner, Dhuleep Singh? You are sure of that?"

"Yes, sir," Grant repeated, his face pale, his distress obvious.

"Thank you. That's all," Narraway said quietly. He hesitated, on the edge of apology, and missed the chance.

Busby declined to ask Grant anything further. His expression reflected his disgust.

It was all hanging on one gamble now. Narraway stood up again. "I would like to call Major Rawlins back, sir."

"Is that really necessary, Lieutenant?" Latimer asked wearily.

"Yes, sir. I believe he may be able to complete my defense of Corporal Tallis, sir," Narraway answered. The hope was taking firmer and clearer shape in his mind all the time. If he was wrong, then there really was nothing left to say.

Latimer agreed. There was a long, tense silence while someone went to find Rawlins. Narraway remained standing, simply because he was too tense to sit down. He did not dare look at Tallis. It was possibly cowardly of him, but the hope was so close, and yet still so far-fetched, that he did not dare offer it.

Busby sat back in his chair, making no secret of his impatience and his contempt. He fidgeted, moved papers, twisted around to see if Rawlins was coming yet.

Latimer waited without moving or looking at either of the officers who sat with him. His dark face was haggard.

The seconds crawled by.

Finally Rawlins arrived. Everyone sat up straighter at once.

Rawlins was reminded of his oath and his position, and he waited, clearly surprised, to hear what Narraway wanted of him now. He too avoided looking at Tallis.

Narraway picked his words with intense care. Everything he said might hold the key to a man's life. He cleared his throat.

"Major Rawlins, you described the injuries Chuttur Singh had received. I don't wish you to do so again. Please just confirm that they were as you told us before. He was struck on the head, but not seriously enough to kill him, just to stun him. And his body was slashed with deep sword wounds from which he bled profusely, so much so that his uniform was sodden with blood. Is that accurate?"

Rawlins's face was tight, bleak with the memory. "Yes."

"He bled to death?" Narraway said.

"I've already said that." Rawlins was angry. "And there was nothing I could have done to save him. To suggest otherwise is not only ridiculous, it is offensive to the three men who found him."

"That would be Grant, Attwood, and Peterson?" Narraway asked. He was aware of an electric tension in the room, almost a prickling. Any moment now, Busby was going to interrupt and break the spell. "Doctor?" he prodded urgently.

"Yes!" Rawlins snapped.

"And those men went after Dhuleep, to see if they could recapture him?"

"Yes!" Rawlins was all but shouting.

"Then who was it who brought the body of Chuttur Singh to you?" Narraway's mouth was so dry he could barely form the words clearly, and yet his body was covered with sweat.

Rawlins froze.

There was a silence in the room that was somehow suffocating.

"Oh, God!" Rawlins cried in horror. "It was a Sikh . . . It . . ."

Narraway licked his lips and forced his voice to be steady. "Could it have been Dhuleep Singh, Major Rawlins?"

Rawlins had known what he was going to say. He stared back at him with eyes wide in his ashen face.

"Yes, it could have been."

Busby sat upright, staring.

Latimer leaned forward, looking first at Rawlins, then at Narraway.

Narraway swallowed hard.

"Sir," he said to Latimer. "I suggest that there is an alternative answer to this tragedy. John Tallis is innocent, as he has always claimed. The assumption that he is guilty arises only from the lack of any other answer."

Now Busby was on his feet. "Are you saying Dhuleep made his own escape, without Tallis's help? That's ridiculous! How did he get out? He was gone before Grant, Attwood, or Peterson even got there."

"No," Narraway said firmly. "No, he was not." He turned back to Latimer. "What if Dhuleep Singh tricked Chuttur, feigning an illness, offering information, or anything else? Then, when he had the opportunity, he struck Chuttur on the head and took his sword and keys. Then when he had killed him, he—"

"In that case, he still couldn't have opened the door, Lieutenant, before Grant got there!" Busby interrupted.

"No," Narraway said again. "You're right. But what if Chuttur was stripped of his guard's uniform and left concealed under the pile of bedclothes? The man Grant spoke to, who told him Dhuleep had escaped with vital information, was Dhuleep himself, with blood smeared over his features, wrapped in Chuttur's bloodstained clothes. We all assumed that someone had opened the door from the outside, and Dhuleep had escaped, closing it behind him. But in fact it was Grant who first opened the door."

There was a sigh around the room, but not a soul moved.

"Dhuleep urged Grant and the others to go as quickly as possible. As soon as they had done so, he took off Chuttur's blood-soaked clothes, re-dressed him, and took him to Rawlins. Then he slipped out and ran away! There was no third man." He took a deep shuddering breath. "That answers all the questions, sir, and it shows John Tallis to be guilty of nothing more than being the only one in the immediate area who happened to be working alone."

Rawlins rubbed his hand across his brow. "You're right," he said with amazement, and with a relief so intense his body shook with it, the color surging back into his face. "I barely looked at the man who brought Chuttur in; I had all my attention on the injured man. But he was definitely Sikh. And the only person unaccounted for other than Tallis was Dhuleep Singh." His voice gained strength and urgency. "But we thought Dhuleep had gone. Of course the three who went looking for him didn't catch him—he was behind them! He went out of the hospital door, in the opposite direction, and got clean away." Rawlins looked across at Tallis. "I'm sorry, John. I was so bloody horrified at what had been done to Chuttur, I never more than glanced at the man who brought him to me."

"He was counting on that," Narraway observed. Then he faced Latimer. "Sir, I respectfully request that

Corporal John Tallis be found not guilty of any wrong-doing at all. There is no villain here."

Slowly Latimer smiled, the light coming back into his eyes, the color to his face. He straightened in his chair and looked first to the man on his right, then the man on his left. Each one nodded, smiling.

"Thank you, Lieutenant Narraway," he said quietly. "This Court finds Corporal John Tallis not guilty in any way whatsoever." He looked at Tallis. "You are free to go, Corporal."

Tallis tried to stand, but he was too weak with the sudden, almost unbelievable turn in his fortunes, and his legs folded under him.

Strafford walked across the courtroom to Narraway, holding out his hand.

"Strafford Minor was wrong about you," he said with intense, burning pleasure. "You're a damn good soldier. There won't be a man or woman in the regiment who isn't grateful to you for this. You've given us back a belief in ourselves. Happy Christmas."

Narraway felt tears sting his eyes. "Thank you, sir. Happy Christmas to you also. I feel a bit more like celebrating now. In fact, I'll go and put some decorations up in my quarters. I've got a blue paper garland I want to hang somewhere special."

Strafford did not ask him to explain. Not that Narraway would have. He simply took the lieutenant's hand and clasped it, so hard he all but crushed his fingers.

"Thank you," he said again. "Happy Christmas."

ABOUT THE AUTHOR

ANNE PERRY is the bestselling author of nine earlier holiday novels—*A Christmas Homecoming, A Christmas Odyssey, A Christmas Promise, A Christmas Grace, A Christmas Journey, A Christmas Visitor, A Christmas Guest, A Christmas Secret,* and *A Christmas Beginning*—as well as the William Monk series and the Charlotte and Thomas Pitt series set in Victorian England, five World War I novels, and a work of historical fiction, *The Sheen on the Silk*. She lives in Scotland.

www.anneperry.com

ABOUT THE TYPE

This book was set in Century Schoolbook, a member of the Century family of typefaces. It was designed in the 1890s by Theodore Low DeVinne of the American Type Founders Company, in collaboration with Linn Boyd Benton. It was one of the earliest types designed for a specific purpose, the *Century* magazine, because it was able to maintain the economies of a narrower typeface while using stronger serifs and thickened verticals.